To the Copper Country

Mihaela's Journey

Barbara Carney-Coston

Wayne State University Press
Detroit

ISBN 978-0-8143-4363-0 (paperback)
ISBN 978-0-8143-4364-7 (e-book)

Library of Congress Control Number: 2017941375

Wayne State University Press
Leonard N. Simons Building
4809 Woodward Avenue
Detroit, Michigan 48201-1309

Visit us online at wsupress.wayne.edu

In loving memory of my mother, Kathryn Lucas Carney,
who told me the stories.

1886

TO THE COPPER COUNTRY

Mihaela's Journey

AUSTRO-HUNGARIAN MONARCHY

GERMAN EMPIRE

PORT OF BREMEN

CROATIA

N E W S

CALUMET, MICHIGAN

NEW YORK CITY

CHICAGO, ILLINOIS

UNITED STATES OF AMERICA

ATLANTIC OCEAN

To the Copper Country

Mihaela's Journey

Great Lakes Books

A complete listing of the books in this series can be found online at wsupress.wayne.edu

Contents

Author's Note   *iii*

Pronunciation of Names and Places   *v*

Translations from Croatian   *vii*

1. Distant Whistles   1

2. Reunion in Red Jacket   9

3. Pasties and Chamomile   17

4. Settling In   25

5. Boardinghouse Chores   29

6. Cooking and Cleaning   35

7. *Tamburica* Time   41

8. New Plants and New Worries   47

9. A Trip into Town   51

10. Post Office and Rain   61

11. Into the Forest   67

12. A School Visit   71

13. Bees   75

14. Discovery   81

15. Unsettled   85

16. *Povitica*   89

17. Birthday News   95

Historical Images from the Copper Country   101

Family Recipes   108

Recommended Books for Young Readers   115

Annotated Bibliography   117

Image Credits   125

Acknowledgments   127

Author's Note

The late nineteenth century was a time of great immigration to the United States for numerous groups of people. They left homes in Europe and elsewhere because of famine, bleak job prospects, or civil unrest in their own countries. Many expected to return to their home countries. But sometimes that didn't happen. The hard work of adjusting to a new life in a strange land took on even more meaning as immigrants mourned old ways and tried to move forward.

In the 1880s, my great-grandfather lived with his extended family on a small farm in Croatia, a beautiful country across the Adriatic Sea from Italy. The Croatian people have been part of different nations over the past 150 years because of wars and political strife. Croatia was then part of the Austrian Empire, and my great-grandfather was labeled "Austrian" on his travel papers. But he and all the people who lived in that area considered themselves to be part of a Slavic group called Croats.

As the family grew and the farm was not able to feed everyone, there was talk that one of the young men might try to earn money somewhere else. Traders passing through their village told about work available in the copper mines near Lake Superior in Michigan's Upper Peninsula. After much family discussion and the offer of a ship ticket from his father-in-law (to be repaid), my great-grandfather decided he would be the one to journey across the sea to America. He traveled to Michigan alone, leaving behind his wife and children, because he didn't expect to stay long. But while he was working in the mines, he developed an eye disease that the local doctors couldn't cure. His wife, my great-grandmother, was highly regarded in their Croatian village for her knowledge of herbs and remedies and other healing skills. There were no antibiotics at that time, and my great-grandmother's abilities were vital to the family's health. My great-grandfather sent a letter asking that his wife come to Michigan and bring her best cures with her. Along with the letter, he included enough money for her to take along their children, too.

In 1886, my great-grandmother left the farm in Croatia with her children and traveled to the German port of Bremen. There, they boarded a ship and spent a difficult voyage crossing the Atlantic Ocean. After they arrived in New York City, they traveled west across several states and north to the Copper Country in Michigan, where they began an unexpected life.

This book is based on my family's history. I grew up in Michigan and spent many happy summer days in the northern part of the state, surrounded by beautiful woods and cold, deep lakes. It was during those days that I began to learn about my background from family members. Numerous details in the story are drawn directly from accounts told to me by my grandparents and my mother. Family reunions provided me with additional exposure to Croatian music, dance, and food. I also did extensive research to verify as many facts as I could.

Numerous Americans today share a similar story of relatives who have come to the United States from other places around the world looking for a better life. After reading this book, I hope you ask about your own family history.

Pronunciation of Names and Places

Andrej (The *j* sounds like a long *i*)

Blaž (The Croatian pronunciation sounds like "Blahs," but our family uses a long *a*, which sounds like "Blaze")

Croatia (Crow-A-sha)

Dijana (The *j* is silent; sounds like "Diana")

Franc Dresich (DRES-ich)

Ida (EE-da)

Josip (YO-sip)

Keweenaw (Native American word pronounced "KEY-win-awe")

Levak (LEV-ak)

Luka (LOO-ka)

Mihaela (Mee-hi-ala) (Current Croatian pronunciation, but our family uses a long *a*, which sounds like "Mee-HAY-la")

Petar (PAY-ter)

Slovenia (The Croatian pronunciation is "Slow-VAN-ee-a")

Tereza (Te-RAZE-a)

Valerija (The *j* is silent; sounds like "Valeria")

Vlado (VLAH-doh)

Translations from Croatian

Asteraceae (Latin)	Aste-RAYS-E-E	Aster plant family
Baba	(BAH-ba)	grandmother
Da	(dah)	yes
dobro jutro	(DO-bro YU-tro)	good morning
domaćinstvo	(do-ma-CHEENST-vo)	household
doviđenja	(do-vid-JANE-ya)	good-bye
hvala	(ha-WA-la)	thank you
idi spavati	(ee-dee-SPA-va-tee)	go to sleep
laku noć	(LA-koo noch)	good night
pauza	*(POW-za)*	halt, pause
pirus (Latin)	(PIE-rus)	pear
povitica	(pova-TEET-za)	nut bread, either sweet or savory
sarma	(SAR-ma)	sour cabbage leaves filled with ground beef, onions, and rice
slatkis	(SLAT-kish)	candy
sretan rođendan	(sret-an ROAD-jen-dan)	happy birthday
tamburica	(tambur-IT-za)	Croatian stringed musical instrument
quercus (Latin)	(Kwer-cus)	oak

To the Copper Country
Mihaela's Journey

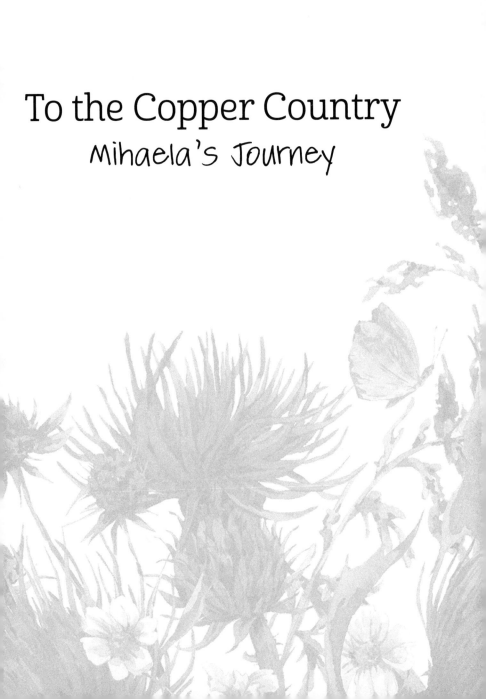

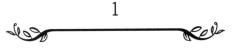

Distant Whistles

Mihaela's heart raced faster than the train rumbling along the tracks. A letter from her father, faded and wrinkled, lay in her lap. She had read it a hundred times since leaving Croatia, but she read it once again.

Houghton County, Michigan
15 August, 1886

Dear Family,
    I have asked a new mining friend to write for me today. Life here in the Copper Country continues as before, with one change. My eyes are worse. I have seen the local doctor, but his medicine isn't working. Please come to Michigan and bring all your best herbs and remedies to help me, or I fear I may go blind . . .

Humid air blew in from the train's open windows. The sun hung low in the sky, illuminating golden fields. Tall grasses near the tracks rippled like water in the wind, while farmers at a distance guided teams of horses pulling plows. Mihaela thought of her uncles back on the farm in Croatia and wondered how they were managing the meager harvest. A drought had made the crops shrivel and the tomatoes and peppers in the garden droop. Could Cousin Katarina carry enough buckets of water from the well to help? Was she was able to get enough milk from the weary old cows? The aunts would cluck like their scrawny hens if that bucket wasn't full. She wondered how any of them would survive if Papa wasn't able to work in the Michigan copper mines and send money home.

She stared at her younger brother sitting across from her. Luka's shirt was untucked and his brown hair stuck up in clumps. He gave her a little wave.

"After we got on the train, I slept for a while," Luka said. "But you slept a long, long time. We passed lots of farms, bigger than ours."

Mihaela didn't respond.

"The conductor kept coming through. Once, he even let me try on his hat."

Mihaela just nodded.

"What's wrong, Mihaela?"

She sunk lower into her seat. "I lost the herb basket at the train station in New York. If Papa's eyes don't get better, it will be my fault."

Luka scratched his head. "But I thought you saved some of the herbs."

"Some. But they may not be the right ones. And there may not be enough of them."

He grimaced.

"Did Mama say anything while I was asleep?" Her mother dozed in the seat next to her youngest brother. Blaž cuddled against Mama and snored softly.

"No," Luka said. "She just seemed sad."

Mihaela's shoulders slumped.

"Maybe you can find more herbs when we get to Michigan." Luka squirmed and fidgeted. "I'm tired of sitting. Do you want to come explore with me?"

Mihaela shook her head and Luka shuffled down the aisle.

She stared out the window, unseeing. Could the woods and meadows in Michigan hold the same kinds of plants as Croatia? She wrapped her arms around her head, curling into a tight ball, and tried to stop thinking about what had happened after the difficult ocean passage.

A ferry had taken them from the huge ship to a crowded dock, and they were herded into a dank building for immigration processing. She was still wobbly from the rough voyage when they were jammed into long lines, waiting to be examined for lice and disease. A doctor had even peeled back their eyelids with a shoe-button hook to look for infection. Then they needed to prove they had some money and tickets to a destination before they could be admitted into the United States. Finally, they had to make their way through the busy city to the train that would take them to Michigan. But the depot was so huge and there were so many people! Somehow, between buying sandwiches and getting a cart for their baggage, she had lost the basket of herbs Mama had handed her.

She had tried to retrace her steps through the cavernous hall. When at last she found the basket, it was broken and sticking out of a trash bin. A man helped her retrieve it, but most of the herbs had fallen into dirty liquid and floor sweepings. All the lavender, rosemary, and St. John's wort were gone, as well as the willow bark and other herbs that had been carefully chosen to treat Papa. Just a few precious bunches of chamomile and peppermint could be saved.

If only she could go back in time to her secret place in the woods! She remembered sitting beneath a beech tree, checking mushrooms to make sure they were safe to eat. She would look at the pictures and writing in the book Mama used to teach her about plants and herbs. The handmade book held drawings and notes that had been passed down from mother to daughter for generations in her family. Mama had given her the book on her last birthday, since tradition held it was hers once she turned eleven. She had even convinced Mama to bring her along on this trip because she was sure she had learned enough to help Papa. Instead, she had lost the herbs meant to cure him.

Shadows on the fields had deepened to a dark purple when Mihaela finally opened her eyes again.

Mama leaned across the train seat. "You've been sleeping for hours. You haven't eaten in so long."

Mihaela shrugged.

Mama offered her a roll, then caught Mihaela's hand in hers. She held it for a moment. "The herbs you saved might be enough."

Mihaela's eyes filled as she looked down at her mother's hands. Everyone said they were big hands for a woman. Strong hands for chopping wood or digging in the garden. Powerful hands, but gentle when brushing hair or wiping a nose. Mama had even set broken bones with her hands.

Mihaela looked at her own hands. Nothing like Mama's.

She chewed her roll slowly as she held back tears. The roll stuck in her throat as she tried to swallow, and her stomach churned. "I'm going to the washroom."

Mama nodded and stared straight ahead, lost in thought.

The lavatory was at the end of the car. There were no long lines of people waiting to use it as there had been on the ship, and when she opened the door, the small space inside was clean. A mirror hung above a basin. She turned on the spigots and fresh water gushed. Flipping her braids over her shoulders, she cupped her hands and splashed water onto her hot face. Her reflection in the mirror showed that the color she usually had from working outside on the farm had faded, and her blue eyes seemed a little grayer. Would Papa recognize her after two whole years? Drying her face with her sleeve, she brushed a few crumbs from her worn dress and left the compartment.

She turned away from the direction she had come. Maybe a walk would help her feel better. Pushing through a door that led onto a platform, warm air blasted around her. The railbed zoomed by underneath the space between the cars. She paused and braced her feet so she could sway with the motion of the train. The clattering on the tracks roared in her ears as she passed through the next compartment. People sprawled over their seats, dressed in threadbare clothes, like hers. Flies buzzed across open wrappers of food. Half-eaten crusts of bread and chunks of smelly cheese didn't make her hungry.

She kept walking. After several more cars, she came to one with patterned carpet on the floor. Men wore suits and ties, and ladies had on fancy dresses trimmed in lace with pretty buttons and bows. They sat in plush chairs at tables covered with white cloths. Men in fitted jackets served them food. Now her stomach felt better, and her mouth watered when she saw thick bowls of soup and plates piled high with chops and potatoes. Delicious smells wafted around her, and she tried not to stare at the people eating. An older man glared at her as he stabbed his meat with a sharp knife.

A conductor beckoned to Mihaela. He took her by the arm, saying something she couldn't understand, and led her back to the car where Mama and her brothers remained.

The conductor leaned over, pointing his thumb toward the window. "Chicago." He spoke in a louder voice and gestured. "Change trains."

"*Da?*" Mama sat up straight. She found the luggage tickets and gave them to him. He waited for a moment, seeming to expect something, then scowled as he left.

The city came into view. Buildings as tall as the ones she had seen near the port in New York towered into the sky. Their windows reflected the bright summer sun. The train's whistle sounded as they pulled into the station, and she thought for a moment of Katarina. The special whistling sound they used to call each other for chores or fun seemed a distant memory now.

A conductor called out to passengers in the car. The English words made no sense to her, but Mihaela knew what was expected. She followed Mama and her brothers, moving automatically. Down the steps, collect the bags, cross the platform, then board the next train—the train that would finally take them to Papa in Michigan.

Steel beams arched high above her, and crowds of people lugged trunks and possessions. Mihaela stared straight ahead and kept walking.

The next train didn't have as many cars. A brass bell sat on top of the engine, and metal spokes on its front jutted out over the track. Bursts of steam billowed from beneath the engine's carriage and seeped out along the rails through waves of heat. They found their way into a passenger car, and a new conductor came to store their luggage.

As they traveled north, air flowing through the open windows turned cooler and fragrant. Mihaela smelled familiar pine and damp earth as she recognized many trees that looked just like the ones in Croatia. Clusters of evergreens with short green needles followed dense forests filled with broad, leafy oaks. Here and there along the track, men worked in the forest. They wielded heavy axes or big, wide saws. Her secret place in the forest at home haunted her.

Luka bounced on his seat. "How much longer?"

Mama looked at the watch hanging around her neck. "We'll be there tomorrow."

"*DA!*" shouted Luka, bouncing higher. "Almost done!"

"*Da!*" said Blaž, copying Luka.

Part of the wooden seat pulled down to make a sleeping space. Mihaela helped Mama gather their hand-knit blankets, brought from home. The hard seats were uncomfortable, but their tickets let them sit in only one section.

Just one more night until I see Papa. Excitement overwhelmed her, but fear, too.

She didn't think there would be much sleeping for any of them tonight.

2

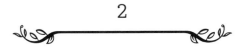

Reunion in Red Jacket

Mihaela stretched and rubbed her eyes as a conductor passed through the car. She heard gulls screech and saw water glimmer in the distance. Was that the Great Lake Papa mentioned in one of his letters? There were just a few passengers left on the train now. She positioned her hands like the Michigan peninsulas, the same way Mama had shown her. She held her right hand palm open, like a mitten with a thumb, and her left hand above it, with her little finger on top, sticking up. She wiggled her little finger. They were headed to the upper part of that finger, the Keweenaw Peninsula.

The conductor motioned their stop was next. "Red Jacket-Calumet!" he called out.

Mihaela knew it was the place Papa would meet them. She strained to look out the window. Her view was partially blocked, and all she could see was a green station house and a church steeple rising behind it.

The whistle sounded, and the train began to slow down. With a great clanging of brakes and a rush of steam, the train came to a stop.

Mihaela picked up her bag and followed her mother and brothers. A few other passengers were in front of them, so they waited to descend the metal steps onto the platform. Her heart pounded. She was about to see her father after two long years! She looked over the heads of her brothers and scanned the crowd—burly men with broad backs, and women and children lined up to meet family or friends. Then, suddenly, she spotted him. He was wearing a shirt that Mama had made. His thick, black hair and his bushy moustache looked just the same.

But red, puffy lids shadowed the twinkle in his eyes now.

"Papa!" Mihaela shouted. "Papa, here we are!"

He waved and ran over to them. Everyone started laughing and crying at the same time. Luka jumped up and down. Mama wiped away tears. Blaž giggled, and Mihaela could hardly breathe.

"Mihaela! You're such a big girl! Tereza! You look beautiful! Boys! How you've grown!" Papa beamed.

"Oh, Papa, your poor eyes!" Mihaela blurted.

Papa's eyes were almost swollen shut.

Mihaela's thumping heart skipped a beat. How could he even see?

"Petar!" Mama embraced him.

Papa hugged Mama tightly as she wiped tears from both of their faces. Then he scooped Mihaela and Luka up into his arms, while Blaž clung shyly to Mama's dress. The two older children squealed as their father gave them bear hugs.

Papa turned to Blaž and squatted down. Blaž shrieked with joy when Papa's thick moustache tickled his cheek.

Everyone began talking at once. There was so much to say!

Papa laughed. "I can't wait to hear everything. But first, let's get your trunks loaded onto the wagon."

Feelings flooded Mihaela. She was so glad to see her father, but concerned, too. "It's nice you can help with these bags,

Papa. It was hard for us to move them around."

"It's wonderful to see you, Mihaela. You're almost grown up." He gave her another hug.

Mihaela loved feeling his strong arms around her. She had to find a way to heal him.

Papa piled the last of their bundles in the wagon and helped them onto the hard plank seats. He snapped the horses' reins, and they set off down the road.

They passed some small frame buildings and the red brick church Mihaela had seen from the train. The wagon turned onto a dirt road that seemed to be taking them away from the town.

Papa snapped the reins again. "We're heading about three miles south, near Osceola. That's also the name of the mine where I work."

Mihaela kept a tight grip on the woven bag that held her herb book and a few other possessions. The thick hand-knit stockings Mama made her wear at the beginning of their journey no longer felt too warm, and she pulled her shawl a little closer.

As the wagon bounced along, sounds of machinery and voices began to fill the air. The clanking noise grew louder when they approached a huge wooden structure. Low buildings connected to a tower that looked like stacked boxes sitting on top of each other. Men covered in mud and dirt milled about.

"Papa, what's this?" Mihaela asked.

"The entrance to one of the copper mines. That's the one I've been working in." Papa pulled up on the reins and the horses slowed down. "It's called a shaft mine. The copper lies deep underground. We dig from different levels, connected to the main passage."

"How do you get down there?" Luka asked.

"We get transported below on something like a moving ladder."

Mihaela tried to imagine such a thing. "Is it dark underground?"

"Very dark. The mining company gives us big lanterns, and I have a special helmet I wear that holds a candle. That way, I can almost see what I'm doing." Papa turned to Mama. "I think the long days underground with all the dirt and rock dust have caused my eye problems. Many injuries to other men, too. If you can cure me, I'll be one of the lucky ones."

Mama hesitated for just a moment, then patted his arm. "We'll do our best."

Mihaela noticed Mama's hand shook a little, but she still had more questions she wanted to ask. "Papa, what do you do with the copper once you mine it?"

Papa grunted. "There are many steps before copper turns into something useful, like wire or pots or roofs for buildings. We use drills to get at the copper in the rock. Then it goes to the stamp mill, where water helps separate the copper from the rock. After that, the copper is heated, or smelted. Smelting makes it liquid. The liquid copper is poured into molds of different sizes. When it cools, it becomes solid again, and those solid pieces are sold by the mining company."

Mihaela tried to picture the process in her head. What heat that must take!

Not far past the mine entrance, they came to a small clearing at the edge of the woods.

"Here we are," Papa said.

Mihaela gawked at where they would be staying. It was so different from their house in Croatia! Instead of having stucco walls and a tile roof, this house was made of logs. Mihaela could even see knobs on the logs where branches had been sawed away. And instead of having crop fields and a garden nearby, this house was nestled close to pine trees.

"The house and land are owned by the mining company, and we pay to rent it. Come, everyone, see what the fellows and I have done on the inside," Papa said.

"What fellows?" Mihaela asked.

But Papa had already gone into the house.

Mihaela stepped inside a large room with a kitchen off the main area. Steps led up to a loft. The floor was wood, not dirt like back home. Sturdy chairs sat around a long table. A rocking chair sat in a corner. A band of men stood awkwardly, smiling and nodding. Mihaela counted. There were twelve of them.

Mama came in. She seemed startled to see the men, too, and pulled Papa aside. "Who are they?" Her whisper was loud enough for Mihaela to hear.

"The boarders." Papa beamed.

"The boarders?"

"Didn't the letter tell you about the boarders? I told him to put that in," Papa said.

"No letter said anything about boarders." Mama frowned.

Papa cleared his throat. The men shifted where they stood,

smiled wider. "A boardinghouse, Tereza. We work with men from many different countries—Italy, England, Ireland . . . and until now we have had to live with Germans and Finns. These men are all from Slovenia. We feel more at home with each other because our languages are similar enough that we can understand each other. We are still the only Croats here."

"And I'm to run this boardinghouse?" Mama's face turned red. She started to speak again but stopped abruptly.

Mihaela could not believe what she had heard. They would be living with these men? These strangers?

Mama walked into the other room, then came back to where everyone waited. She drew a deep breath and crossed herself. "I cook over an open fire at home. Can someone show me how to use the stove? I need a cup of tea."

Everyone crowded into the kitchen. The boarders fell all over each other as they scrambled to assist her.

"The wood goes in here, see?" said one boarder. "And then you light it, close the door, and before you know it, you have a nice, hot oven."

"She wants tea, remember?" said another. "Mrs. Levak, these are the burners. You lift them up with this poker, and put wood in here, and light it. Then you put the kettle on top, and soon it boils. But first, we need water. The well and pump are just out the back door. I will go." He was back quickly with a large bucket of water.

"I'm thirsty," Luka said.

Another boarder poured water from the bucket into a nearby pitcher and then found a cup for Luka.

"So cold, it hurts my teeth!" Luka held out his cup. "But good. More, please."

"That water comes from a spring fed by the biggest Great Lake," Papa said. "Superior never warms up, not even in summer. Who else wants some?"

Mihaela and Blaž drank a cup of the cold water, too.

A tall, thin man stepped forward. "My name is Andrej. Pleased to meet you, Mrs. Levak." He did a little bow. "Petar told us you like tea, so we got plenty of it." A glass container for tea sat next to others filled with flour, sugar, and salt.

At least most of the boarders seemed nice. Mihaela saw there was even a jar filled with walnuts—for her favorite bread, *povitica*?

Mama took a deep breath. "I hope you understand this is a big shock for me. I had no idea."

One of the boarders handed her a cup of tea. Then the men excused themselves and left the cabin.

"Where are they going?" Luka asked.

"They're giving us a little time to get reacquainted," Papa said.

Mama sat at the kitchen table looking around her. Her shoulders sagged, and she started to weep.

Papa looked distraught. "Tereza, I'm sorry. I thought you knew . . . if I could have written my own letter, there wouldn't have been any confusion."

Mama wiped her eyes. "I'm relieved that we're finally here. But I'm stunned at . . . the circumstances." She took a sip of her tea. "I'm supposed to cook and clean for all these strangers?"

"Yes, but they will pay you. For food, laundry, and expenses,"

Papa said.

"They will pay me?" Mama's eyes widened.

Mihaela hung on every word as her parents talked.

"And what do expenses include, besides food?" Mama asked.

"Not much. Whatever else you might need to run the household. The rest is ours to keep."

"Twelve hardworking men will eat a lot of food."

"The going rate is three dollars per man, per month. If it's not enough, we'll ask them to pay a little more."

Mama shook her head. "I have never been paid for my work before."

Papa nodded slowly. "With both of us earning money for the family, we have a real chance. And now that you all are here, we will be able to help each other."

Mihaela took another big gulp of water. How would they all live together? Where would everyone sleep? Would they share meals? They were only supposed to stay until Papa was well, so did this mean they would be staying longer? Mama didn't seem to like the idea of running a boardinghouse, either. What a shock for all of them! But more money would help the family. Mihaela thought of her chores in Croatia. She knew how to milk a cow and weed the garden. What would be expected of her here?

She wiped her upper lip with the back of her hand.

Helping to cure Papa's eyes had to be her first job.

3

Pasties and Chamomile

Mihaela couldn't get enough of the ice-cold water, and she helped herself to another cup. Loud growls sounded from her stomach.

"Mihaela, what's that I hear?" Papa asked. "Do you feel all right?"

"Yes, Papa. I have the family's loudest stomach. The water tastes wonderful, it's just sloshing around in my empty belly."

Papa slapped his hand to his forehead. "You're hungry." He took a plate covered by a cloth from the back of the stove and set it on the kitchen table.

"Petar, we need to wash up first," Mama said. "We're pretty grimy."

Papa gestured toward the pitcher and basin near the back door. "And the privy is out back."

Everyone lined up and found strong soap and a scratchy towel. Then the Levak family sat down for their first meal together in over two years.

Papa cleared his throat and bowed his head. "Dear God, we give thanks for the safe arrival of my family, and for this food."

"Amen." Mihaela licked her lips.

Papa took off the towel that had been covering the platter, and a delicious odor filled the room.

"What's that?" Mihaela stared at something shaped like a half moon and flaky, with an edge to the crust that was braided like rope.

"They're called pasties," Papa said. "The miners from Cornwall, in Great Britain, eat these. A few of them that work in the mines here shared them one day, and everyone tasted how good they were. Now all the miners eat pasties for our noon meal. The cook who makes them carves our initials in the dough so we know who gets what before they go into our lunch buckets. Sometimes, we heat them up on the backs of our shovels in the mine furnace. Our former boarding missus, the lady we used to live with, sent these over."

Mihaela's mouth watered as Mama put one on each of their plates.

"Be careful," Papa said. "They stay hot inside for a long time."

Mihaela bit into her pasty, and steam rose from the rich crust. She tasted diced potatoes, rutabagas, onions, and small pieces of tender beef. It was delicious.

After blowing hard to cool it off, Luka jammed half the pasty into his mouth. He smiled as he chewed and swallowed, gulping it down. He ate the second half almost as fast, then took a breath and held out his plate. "Another, please?"

"Already?" Mama laughed.

"*Da!*"

"The boy could use a little meat on his bones," Papa said.

"Luka was seasick more than the rest of us," Mama said. "Thank God he's still healthy. There were many children on board who wasted away."

Papa glanced around the table. "I know how hard it must have been for you all."

Mihaela looked at her father's swollen eyes. She swallowed hard, but not because of the pasty.

Mama turned to Papa. "You say these pasties were made by the woman you used to board with?"

"Yes, Mrs. Milcher. We're still paying her to make them until you get settled. She's a good soul. She wanted to let you know that you are welcome here."

"Do all the boardinghouses provide a noon meal for the men to take to the mines? As well as breakfast and dinner?" Mama asked.

Mihaela's ears pricked up. Did Mama's voice have an edge?

"That's the custom," Papa said.

Mama didn't say anything, but a frown shot across her brow.

Mihaela tried to concentrate on her food as she told Papa details about their voyage—having to sleep next to strangers, the terrible smells onboard, the big storm that caused Mama to bump her head as the ship listed, and a girl she had met named Valerija. "We played with our dolls together. It helped us pass the time. Nine days at sea felt like forever."

"How big was your ship?" Papa asked.

"Huge!" Luka said.

"Over a thousand passengers," Mama added. "When we got to the port in Bremen, it was overwhelming. But . . . we managed." She grew quiet again.

"I am so grateful you're all here," Papa said. He turned to Mama. "What do you think about my eyes? Did you bring your best remedies?"

It was the moment Mihaela had been dreading ever since

she arrived. She held her breath.

Mama looked at Mihaela, then at Papa. "We have some herbs that I hope will help. Why don't you show the boys where they're going to sleep, while Mihaela and I get things ready."

Mihaela exhaled slowly as she pulled hard on her braids. She was relieved that Mama hadn't told Papa how the basket of herbs had been lost. But she was stunned at how bad her father's eyes looked.

As Papa led Blaž and Luka off to see their room, Mama leaned across the table and spread out the cloth that had covered the pasties. On it, she placed the dried plants they had managed to save. One bundle was still wrapped in fabric. "Papa's eyes are . . . worse than I thought. We'll just have to see what we can do." She stood and put a kettle on the stove to boil. Inside a cupboard, she found a bowl and a knife and put them on the table. Then she picked up the smallest bundle of herbs and handed them to Mihaela. "Crumble these dried chamomile flowers as finely as you can and put them in the bowl. I'll be right back."

Mihaela stared at the herbs and said a prayer while she ground them between her fingers. Her nose twitched as the pungent scent filled the air.

Mama returned carrying her best nightgown.

Mihaela had never seen her wear it, but she and Katarina had often looked at it in the trunk that held Mama's few special possessions. It was made of soft, fine wool and decorated with lace. Mihaela knew Mama had crocheted the lace herself.

The kettle finally started to boil. Mama poured hot water

into the bowl filled with the crushed chamomile. She picked up the knife and poked the blade tip through the hem of the nightgown to loosen a thread. Then, she started to rip the garment into long strips.

"Mama, stop! What are you doing?"

"It's all right," Mama said quietly. "We need to soak strips of cloth in the mixture, and then apply them to Papa's eyes. The cloth must be very clean."

"But, Mama, it's . . ."

" . . . just a nightgown. I can make another."

"Can you save the lace?"

"Yes. I can do that. The lace will not soothe his eyes." Mama used the knife blade again to pick a few threads from the collar that ran around the neck of the garment. She gently pulled the lace away. Then she tore what was left of the fabric in half and handed one piece to Mihaela. "Keep tearing this into thin strips. We'll need many before we're done."

Mihaela hesitated for a moment. Mama had taught her about herbs and plants and even how to read and write. She realized Mama was not giving her a simple lesson, but a deep and silent one. She hated to do it, but she started to rip. "How long do these herbs need to steep?"

Mama looked into the bowl. She bent over and inhaled. "It's almost ready. Go get Papa."

Mihaela walked through the main room of the cabin, passing the rough, wooden chairs near a large fireplace at one end of the room. Smooth, gray rocks surrounded the hearth and continued up the chimney. A mantel over the fireplace held a rectangular clock that made a quiet ticking sound. A black wire screen stood in front of the hearth, where white wisps curled up from a few dying embers. Next to it was a pail filled with ashes. A small shovel and a big basket of sticks rested nearby. Mihaela sniffed a memory. She hadn't smelled the scent of burning wood since she left Croatia.

"Mihaela?" Papa had come into the room.

Mihaela jumped, startled.

"You were far away, eh?"

"Yes, sorry, Papa." Mihaela lingered. "The smell of smoke reminded me of home."

Papa nodded. "Smells can bring strong memories."

Mihaela put her hand into her father's. "Mama says it's time to treat your eyes. We have things ready." She led him back into the kitchen.

Mama gestured. "Petar, sit here."

Papa took a seat.

Mama chose one of the strips she had torn and dipped it into the chamomile herb mixture. She wrung it out over the bowl, and then draped the cloth across Papa's eyes.

Mihaela watched, observing everything her mother did.

"Very soothing." Papa tilted his head back a little more.

Mama motioned for Mihaela to dip another strip into the bowl. She took the first cloth from Papa's eyes.

"I'll do the next one," Mihaela said. She wrung out the cloth and gently applied it to her father.

"So, you're learning these skills, too?" Papa asked.

"Trying."

"Mihaela brewed a remedy that was just right when I bumped my head on the ship," Mama said. "I had a concussion. It was her good care that helped me get well enough to pass the health inspection when we went through immigration in New York."

Mihaela remembered how scared she had been then that they wouldn't be admitted into the United States. She was so relieved she had been able to help Mama.

"With both of you here, I'm sure I'll be cured quickly," Papa said.

Mihaela changed the dressing a few more times, then wrapped the remaining herbs in a cloth and put them on a shelf. She was glad Papa's eyes were still covered. He wasn't able to see the worried look on Mama's face.

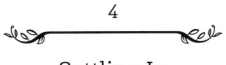

4

Settling In

Mihaela left the kitchen and climbed up split log steps to a loft that held twelve beds, six on each side of the room. Her brothers were already there.

"Mihaela, watch this." Luka jumped from one row of beds to the other.

Blaž had already tried and missed. He rubbed his knee.

Luka hopped from bed to bed. He stopped when Papa appeared.

"This is the boarders' sleeping room," Papa said. "You're not to disturb their things. Now that you've seen it, don't come back up here."

"It looks just like our loft in the *domaćinstvo*," Mihaela said.

"Everyone, come." Papa picked up Blaž. "Mihaela, I need to show you your room."

Mihaela descended the stairs and saw that one part of the wall had the outline of a door. When Papa pushed on a protruding wooden handle, it opened into a small room. The space inside was just big enough to hold a bed and a washstand with a scrap of mirror above. There were pegs on the log walls to hang clothes. A little window let in light. Two fluffy pillows were propped against a log headboard, and a heavy woolen blanket covered the mattress.

Mihaela was amazed. "A room just for me?"

Papa smiled. "*Da.*"

Mihaela hadn't imagined anything like this. She ran her hand over the blanket and touched the soft pillows. The last time she had slept in a real bed she had been with Katarina and her other cousins, crowded together in the loft back home. For a moment, she felt like a princess with a space all her own, almost as private as her secret forest nook.

Bong, bong, bong . . . A chime sounded from the main room.

Mihaela moved toward the fireplace mantel and squinted at the clock. "Is it really nine o'clock? And still light outside?"

Papa nodded. "The clock is right."

"How can that be?" Mihaela asked.

"I can't tell you the scientific reason," Papa said. "But the sun rises and sets here later than back home."

Mihaela pulled on her braids, thinking hard. She wanted to know the answer to that. She wanted to know about everything! "Where did this clock come from? It's beautiful."

"I traded for it. Another lucky miner got one of those wonderful shirts your mother made me." He turned to Mama. "I thought you would need a clock, and it's a good one."

"I do have this." Mama touched the watch hanging around her neck.

"It needs to be wound just once a day," Papa said.

"So lovely. I am honored that one of my shirts could command such a price. And with two timepieces, I will know exactly when I should have dinner ready, eh?"

Papa scratched his neck. "It's hard to wait for the food to cook after a long day in the mines."

"And what about breakfast? What time for that?"

The edge in Mama's voice had returned.

Papa cleared his throat. "A little later than at the *domaćinstvo*."

Mama closed her eyes for a moment and then shook her head. "I think we'd all better turn in soon."

Mihaela couldn't stand their first day together after so long ending like this. "Wait! We told Papa stories. Can't he tell us one?"

Papa looked at Mama and she nodded. "Just for a little while."

They sat down and Blaž climbed onto Papa's lap.

"You've already seen that America is a lot different than Croatia," Papa began.

"Huge buildings in the cities," Mihaela said.

"Different foods," Luka said.

"And here's another difference. Peddlers are not the custom around here like they were in our village. There are many stores in Calumet, not far from the train station."

"What do they sell in the stores?" Mihaela asked.

"Everything! There are butchers and shoemakers, and some stores sell bolts of cloth and readymade clothes. Others sell flour and salt, cheeses and pickles. The biggest pickles you ever saw! They're kept in a big, wooden barrel full of brine."

Mihaela wrinkled her nose and laughed at the mention of giant pickles.

Luka made a smacking sound with his lips.

Papa reached into his shirt pocket and produced a small brown paper package that he slowly unwrapped. He held out five sticks, swirled with red and white. "I almost forgot. One of the things sold in town is *slatkis*." He offered the first to Mama, then one each to Mihaela, Luka, and Blaž.

Blaž noticed there was one left. "Who for?"

"Me!" Papa took a big bite.

Mihaela savored the sweet and spicy flavors of the candy. She had never seen a pretty stick like this. As she licked it, the red on the tip soon disappeared and only a white point was left. Taking a small bite, she let the crunchy bits melt on her tongue. She glanced at her brothers and saw that they had as much sticky red on their faces as in their hands. "When can we go to these stores?"

"Soon," Papa said.

The clock on the mantel chimed once more.

Mama looked up. "Goodness, now it's nine thirty." She stretched. "Children, time for bed. *Idi spavati*."

Mihaela didn't protest this time. After washing her face in her very own basin, she looked around at her very own room, her very own bed. She climbed under the covers and let out a deep sigh as she snuggled beneath her blanket. No rocking ship or snoring passengers. She was finally in Michigan. But seeing Papa's eyes and then learning about the boarders was such a shock. She felt grateful her family was together, and she was happy to have a full stomach, but what was going to happen? Could they manage all the work? Could she help Papa? She reached for Dijana, the carved wooden doll Papa had made for her long ago, and tried to go to sleep. Maybe in the morning, things would make sense.

5

Boardinghouse Chores

Mihaela woke to the sound of a whistle. She thought for a moment she was back on the ship, but when she sat up, there was no rusty, peeling paint or slimy steel beams overhead to avoid. There were no strong smells from tightly packed people or fumes from the ship's engine. She got on her knees to peek out the window. The sun was rising, and the first light revealed pines and birches growing near the cabin. The call of a gull high overhead made her look up. It soared through a ribbon of smoke, drifting into wooly clumps of clouds. Noisy birds had begun squawking before dawn, but she had already been restless, thinking about Papa's eyes.

She lay back down, not wanting to leave her comfortable bed, when a wonderful aroma wafted into her room. Bacon! She flung back the covers and felt the hard wooden floor under her bare feet. Rinsing her mouth with water from the pitcher on the washstand, she looked in the mirror. Her eyes seemed bluer in this light, and her hair darker brown. She quickly braided two plaits and pulled on her dress. Laboring over her stockings and shoes, she managed to fasten the shoe buttons without the shoe hook. Finally ready, she walked into the main room of the cabin.

A few of the boarders were still seated at a long table, finishing their breakfasts. They greeted her cheerfully.

Mihaela opened the door to the kitchen.

"Just in time." Mama and Papa were placing a large platter of eggs and bacon on the table for Luka and Blaž.

"Looks like everyone but me has been up for a while," Mihaela said.

"Papa cooked breakfast this morning. He needed to show me where everything is before he leaves for the mines." Mama seemed a little less tense.

"And I hear the mine whistle again. That means I've got to go. Help your mama today, children."

"Petar . . ." Mama's words faded.

Papa paused. "Tereza, don't worry. I told the men not to expect too much tonight." He gave her a kiss and was gone.

"More eggs, please," said Blaž. His legs dangled from the big chair.

Mama still stared at the door. "Of course, but your sister hasn't had any yet." She handed Mihaela a plate and piled it high with eggs and bacon. Then she gave Blaž another serving. "Luka, how about you?"

"*Da.*" He sucked bits of bacon from his fingers. "What are we going to do today?"

"There will be plenty of work," Mama said. "We'll do the dishes. Then there's food to prepare, laundry to wash, sixteen beds to make . . ."

"Sixteen! Why so many?" Luka made a face.

"Twelve boarders, three children, and one for Mama and Papa," Mihaela answered. "I haven't done sums in a long time." She grew wistful for a moment. "I miss that."

"I'm glad you can still do your arithmetic. We need to have

our lessons again," Mama said. "But these chores come first. It will be my job to make the boarders' beds, and you children will have to make your own, like you did at home. When you're done with your breakfast, Mihaela and Luka, take the bucket hanging there by the door and go and find the pump. Blaž, I have a job just for you."

Mihaela enjoyed every bite on her plate and licked the last crumbs from her lips. It was nice to be able to eat as much as she wanted.

Luka pushed back from the table and retrieved the large wooden bucket, then swung the screen door open.

Mihaela was close behind.

One side of the house had a grassy expanse, ringed by thorny bushes and surrounded by pine trees, with birches to one side. Farther out were dense woods. The other half of the yard glowed in the morning sun, rich with wildflowers that swayed in the breeze. Lacy white stars, yellow petals with big black centers, and pods with purple flowers bobbed gently. Mihaela wondered what they were called here. The lacy ones looked similar to a wildflower they had in Croatia, with a root like a carrot. As she scanned the yard for more plants, she wondered whether any of them could help her father's eyes.

Mihaela walked farther into the yard and heard the soft drone of insects and bees. Shading her eyes with her hands, she saw four tall weathered posts in the middle of the grass. Thin ropes were strung between them, and a lone pair of black socks hung secured by wooden pins. Turning, she noticed the two small huts they had all visited last night, their doors slightly ajar now. The privies would seem far away in bad weather. At least the pump was nearby.

Luka was looking at a bug, so even though he had the bucket, Mihaela was first to the pump. She lifted the handle and began the up and down motion that brought the water gushing.

Luka placed the bucket under the spout just as the water flowed. "I want to do it!" He shoved Mihaela aside to grab the pump handle.

"I was first!" Mihaela cupped her hands and scooped a shower of water onto her brother.

The cold water startled Luka, and he stopped to catch his breath. He reached into the bucket and did the same to Mihaela. They both began to laugh.

The water fight grew until their whoops and screams brought Mama to the door. "What's going on?"

Mihaela grinned. She took the half-full bucket and dumped it over Luka's head.

Luka sputtered.

"Mihaela, enough! Luka, you'll have to wait for your revenge. I need the water. Come!"

"He started it!" Mihaela could see that her mother was trying not to laugh.

"It's finished now. There's work waiting."

Luka flashed an impish smile. "I'll get you later."

Mama watched as they filled the bucket and walked into the house. "You're soaking." She shook her head but didn't scold. "Put the water in that black pot."

They carefully poured it in.

"After you get on dry clothes, you can bring me the dishes from the boarders' table." Mama fed more kindling under the burners. "Be careful. They'll break if you drop them. They're not wood, like our bowls in Croatia."

Mihaela and Luka stopped to look at Blaž. His little hands were working hard. "What's he doing?" Mihaela asked.

"He's tearing up pieces of stale bread to put into the chickens we'll cook for dinner tonight. Papa's idea," Mama said.

"Into the chickens?"

"Yes. Papa says it's because the chickens are baked in the oven, not on a spit over an open fire, like we did at home. He learned about this from Mrs. Milcher. Stuffing, he called it. All the men think it's delicious."

Mihaela shrugged. "The pasties were good. Maybe this will be, too."

"I guess we'll need to try many new foods," Mama said. "Papa also said that the men expect some kind of sweet, but different from our Croatian cakes. I suppose I'll learn to make them. But not today. Now, go and change, then bring me those dishes."

Mihaela put on a green dress that was almost the same as her everyday blue, but a little less shabby. It was the dress she wore to church back home.

Blaž was still tearing bread when Mihaela and Luka returned to the kitchen.

"That's enough stuffing, Blaž," Mama said. "We'll make beds next."

Mihaela had finished smoothing her blanket when she heard a noise overhead and realized that Mama was in the boarders' sleeping loft. Twelve beds to make. She walked to the foot of the steps and called out, "Want some help?"

Mama came to the top of the stairs. "Your father said you weren't to come up here, but if you're with me, I think it would be all right. Yes, I could use the help."

Mihaela joined her mother and they moved from bed to bed, straightening blankets and pillows. The men had few possessions to avoid. Were they sending all their money home to hungry families, too? A chair stood between each bed, and pegs on the log walls held their spare shirt and trousers. Mihaela could see cracks of daylight between the logs that formed the roof. She shivered, imagining what it would be like when the weather turned cold.

As they made the last bed, Mihaela turned to her mother. "Was the chamomile we used last night on Papa's eyes helpful? It's funny to think that something we can drink as a tea can also be used on eyes."

"It can reduce skin irritation." Mama gave the blanket a pull, then hesitated. "But I'm not sure it's helping Papa's eyes. We'll try that again and the other herbs we have, but we probably won't know for a few days."

"What if we don't have the right herbs after all?"

Mama shook her head.

"What about the stores? Maybe they sell things we can use. Or an American doctor?"

"Papa has seen the local doctor."

"Your medicine is better, anyway."

"I hope so." Mama sighed. "We'll just have to wait and see."

6

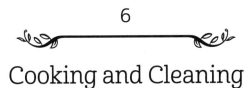

Cooking and Cleaning

Chores needed finishing, and laundry came next.

Mihaela and Luka took turns carrying buckets of water to be heated on the stove. Mihaela helped Mama scrape the dirt from the boarders' overalls in the yard and placed them in the big metal washtub near the door. Mama scrubbed them against a wavy metal washboard until all the grime was gone and rinsed them in a second washtub. Then Mihaela and Luka dragged the heavy, wet garments to the clothesline and hung them in rows.

After the laundry was done, everyone was hungry. On the farm, dinner was always at noon, but here, the main meal was in the evening. Lunch was warmed-over pasties from the night before. Mihaela thought they tasted just as good the second day.

Mama cleared the table when they finished eating and turned to Mihaela and Luka. "We need to start dinner preparations soon. We'll need lots of potatoes and carrots to go with the chickens. There's a root cellar under the house where things are stored. Papa showed it to me this morning before you were awake."

They followed her out the back door. Mihaela saw two plain wooden doors close to the house on an angle to the ground. She went down steps into a small room with a dirt floor. The ceiling was so low that she had to duck her head when she got to the bottom. It was cool and dark in the cellar, but enough light from the open doors let her see burlap sacks full of potatoes and bags of carrots on wooden shelves above the ground.

Mama handed two small sacks of potatoes to Mihaela and Luka, then took one for herself, adding bags of carrots on top.

Mihaela squinted against the bright light as she came up the steps.

Mama arranged her sacks on the kitchen floor. "It's certainly going to take us a while to peel all of these."

Mihaela set her potatoes on the table and got a bowl with water to scrub the vegetables clean. The peeling began. Blaž was in charge of putting the scrapings into a big pot for the start of tomorrow's soup.

After many potatoes, Luka groaned. "I liked my chores in Croatia. Weeding the garden was more fun."

Mihaela's hands and back ached. "Milking the cow with Katarina was better than this." She wondered what her cousin was doing right now.

"At least we have enough to eat here," Mama said. "That's a good change. And think of your cousins. If we are able to send them money, they won't be as hungry, either."

Mihaela did like having a full stomach. She decided not to complain. "How long do the chickens need to cook?"

Mama opened the heavy black door of the oven and wiggled one of the legs of the roasting chickens. "I'm not sure. I'll just have to keep checking." She wiped a trickle of sweat from the side of her face with the back of her hand. "There's one more chore before we can take a break. The tables need to be set."

"Do we eat with the boarders?" Mihaela asked.

"Papa says sometimes we will. For now, it's better if we eat together as a family in the kitchen. We can put all the food on big platters in the center of the table for the boarders. That way, they can help themselves and we don't have to jump up and down to serve them."

After Mihaela set the tables, she went to her room. She hadn't completely unpacked her bag yet, and she shook out one more dress that was reserved for special occasions. It was in the traditional style of her village, with red embroidered ribbon trim. She remembered the last time she had worn it, for Blaž's baptism. Mama had to let out all the seams and the hem before they left Croatia, since she had grown so much taller in the three years since he was born. With the drought, and with Papa leaving, there were no weddings or happy occasions after that. Would they have anything to celebrate here in Michigan? She ran her hand over the ribbon and then hung the dress on one of the wall pegs.

As she checked her bag a final time, she found a smooth piece of bark with a drawing of two girls in a barn. Katarina had given it to her just before they left Croatia, and her pencil had captured all the details—Mihaela's braids getting in the way while she milked the cow, the cat mewing for a taste—even her basket of herbs near the milking stool. Mihaela pressed the drawing to her heart and thought about her cousin. Was she still drawing such fine pictures? She set the bark onto the small table next to the bed. It was hard not to miss Katarina.

She sighed as she reminded herself why they were here. Picking up her herb book, she glanced through it, looking for ideas. Papa was counting on Mama and her for help. Maybe plants she had seen on her way from the train would be like those she knew in Croatia. She turned the pages slowly, studying the drawings and reading the notes. A soft breeze through the open window carried the sound of gulls, and she heard a mine whistle blow. The day had sped by. She put her book aside and went to the kitchen.

Mama took the chickens and vegetables out of the oven just as the men trooped in the back door. Some of the miners had already washed up at the mine changing room and greeted her as they passed by. They eagerly found their seats at the big table.

Papa was the last one to come from the mines. He left his muddy work clothes outside, but bits of dirt still clung to his hair.

Mihaela looked at his face. His eyes didn't seem any better.

Mama scooped the stuffing out of the chickens, then carved them and put the meat onto several platters. She placed a platter on the family table, and carried two more into the main room. Mihaela and Luka helped with the rest.

The boarders passed the food rapidly. The first mouthfuls brought praise for the cooks. "Mrs. Levak, this is wonderful," one of the boarders said. "Petar told us you were a great cook. He was right."

Mama's mouth curled in a slight smile. "I couldn't have done it without my helpers." She gestured to Mihaela and Luka, who stood nearby. "But we didn't have time to make sweets."

The men laughed. "This dinner is so good we don't need any."

"I'll be back in a while," Mama said. "I need to feed my family."

Papa said a blessing, then filled plates.

Blaž grinned at his father as he took a big bite of the stuffing. "Blaž cooked. Tasty!"

Papa laughed. He looked around the table and winked. "The rest of you give Blaž any help?"

Mihaela laughed, too. "Not much." Her hard work was almost worth it. Every bite was delicious.

Luka rolled his eyes. "I peeled a thousand potatoes."

"Good for your muscles." Papa squeezed Luka's arm. "Are you all too worn out to hear a little music tonight?"

Mihaela's eyes lit up. "Will you play your *tamburica*?"

"That's what I'm thinking." Papa got up from the table to check on the men. "Any more food needed?" he asked from the doorway.

"We've had enough, thanks. Wonderful meal," said Josip.

"Josip, how's your fiddle? Andrej, yours, too. We need to celebrate my family being here. What do you say we make a little music tonight?"

"A great idea!" they said.

Some of the other men went to get their instruments.

"We'll wash the dishes later," Papa said.

Mihaela smiled as she stepped into the main room. Even though she was bone weary, tonight she would laugh and have fun!

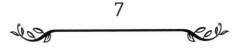

Tamburica Time

Papa found his *tamburica* and began plucking at the gourd-shaped stringed instrument. Josip and Andrej returned with their violins. The other boarders grinned as they looked on. Papa began to strum an old tune that Mihaela had heard often in the *domaćinstvo*. It reminded her of home.

Soon the air was alive with music and tapping feet. The strings hummed as Papa plucked a familiar melody. The men pushed away chairs, and one of the boarders started dancing as the others laughed and whistled.

"Vlado! A leap! Do the leap!"

Vlado was a tall man with blond hair. He gave a slight bow and then leapt into the air, kicking both feet out straight and touching his toes at the same time. The children laughed and applauded.

"My Russian uncle taught me that." Vlado made another bow in front of Mihaela as a new tune began. Mihaela shyly took his extended hand. Round and round they went. He twirled and spun her until she was out of breath. Then he bowed again and danced with Luka and Blaž. When Vlado came to Mama, Papa leapt up from his chair and handed his *tamburica* to him.

"My turn," Papa said.

Vlado laughed and began to pluck the instrument. Vlado wasn't as skilled a player as Papa, but he was good enough.

Mama beamed and put her hand into Papa's. They danced

around the room as everyone stepped back.

Mihaela felt relieved. She hadn't seen her mother smile like that in a long time.

The men played until their faces glistened. "Water!" Josip laughed. "I need to rest!"

Everyone was red-faced and breathing hard when the clock struck nine.

"I had no idea it was so late," Mama said. "Time for the children to be in bed."

"No!" Blaž said. "Not tired!"

"But we are," Vlado said. "We've all had a long day." He wiped his face with the back of his sleeve and turned to Mama. "Mrs. Levak, it's nice to share your family. And thank you for cooking and cleaning for us. I hope my wife and children will soon be able to join me here, too." He started up the stairs to the boarders' sleeping loft.

Mihaela was beginning to like the miners. Still, they were no substitute for her uncles back home.

Mama helped the boys get ready for bed, while Mihaela and Papa returned to the kitchen to wash the dishes.

Papa hummed one of the tunes he had played. "It's wonderful to have you here," he said to Mihaela. "We've played some music, but no one has danced."

"After you left, we didn't do any dancing at home, either." Mihaela looked closely at her father's face. "How do your eyes feel tonight, Papa?"

"About the same. Almost forgot about them with the music."

"Sit, Petar," Mama said, as she came back into the kitchen.

"We need to apply the treatment again. Mihaela, can you get what we need?"

Mihaela quickly retrieved their limited supplies. She crushed more of the chamomile leaves in the bowl while Mama added hot water. Mihaela began sponging Papa's eyes with the cloth strips.

Mama watched. "Maybe we should add a little olive oil to this mixture," she said. "But it has to be very pure. Would the stores have such a thing?"

Papa shifted in his chair. "No doubt they'd have some sort of oil. Ah . . ." He sighed as Mihaela applied the next warm cloth. "I'll have to get a horse and wagon for you. Mihaela, can you see if Josip is still awake out there? His brother might let us use his team again."

Mihaela pushed the door open to the next room. A few of the boarders were talking near the fire. "Yes, he's still there."

"Josip!" Papa called. "Can you come here, please?"

Josip struggled to get out of his chair. One leg dragged a little as he entered the kitchen. "Petar, how are the eyes?"

"My wife and daughter are taking good care of me," Papa said. "But Tereza is going to need more supplies from the stores. Can I hire your brother's horse and wagon on a regular basis?"

"I don't see why not. I'll speak with him about it."

Mama started making a list out loud. "We'll need the oil, and other food, too . . . bacon, butter, flour . . ."

Mihaela's hand went to her forehead.

"What's wrong?" Papa asked.

"We don't know the English words for these things."

"You're right, Mihaela," Mama said. "I'm sure the shopkeeper doesn't speak Croatian. And I may not be able to see what they have to point to it . . ."

"Mrs. Levak, I'll be glad to help you with your shopping list," Josip offered.

"Josip here knows more English than the rest of us put together. Reads and writes a little of it, too. But you need to careful." Papa lifted his bandages to glare at Josip. "He's the one who 'forgot' to write about the boarders in my last letter."

Josip glanced at Mama, then cast his eyes down. "Mrs. Levak, I know I should have, but I was just so worried that you wouldn't want to stay with a bunch of miners like us."

"I'll have to watch what I tell you to say," Mama said. "You won't leave things off my list, will you?"

Josip blushed. "I'll try not to."

Mama looked at Papa's eyes as Mihaela replaced the cloths. "Do you think we can get the horses soon?"

Josip nodded. "I'll talk with my brother in the morning, before work."

Papa grunted while Mihaela applied more compresses to his eyes. "If you do your shopping at P. Ruppe and Son's store, you may not need many English words."

"What do you mean?" Mihaela asked.

"The Ruppes are Slovenian, just like our boarders, and we understand each other pretty well. It won't hurt to have a few English words, though, since some of the clerks at the store are from other places."

Josip lingered until the conversation was over. "Well, I'll say goodnight now."

"*Laku noć*, Josip." Mama shook her head when he left. "So he's the one who chose not to tell me about the boarders in the letter, eh? I certainly didn't expect to take care of so many other men. But it is just for a little while."

Mihaela waited for Papa to agree, but he didn't say a word. And then she remembered something Valerija had told her on the ship: *"Everyone says they'll go back home, but no one does."*

Mihaela thought about that all night long.

8

New Plants and New Worries

Mama finished washing the breakfast pots and pans. "Mihaela, please watch your brothers. I'm going to check some of the wildflowers and other plants I saw growing nearby. I won't be long."

Mihaela put down her book about herbs to help Blaž finish eating a bowl of oatmeal.

Luka reached over and picked up the book. "Did you write these notes and draw these pictures?"

"I wrote a few notes in the back. Most of the writing and pictures are from Mama and Baba and even great-grandmother." Mihaela wiped oatmeal from Blaž's face with a cloth. "I'm adding to it as I learn more."

"The drawings are nice. But some of the words look funny."

Mihaela looked at the page he had opened. "Like *quercus*? That's Latin for 'oak.'"

"Are oaks the trees with acorns?"

"Yes. That's how we make our ink for writing, too. Remember how we boiled the oaks' bark in Croatia, before we left?" She turned to another page and pointed. "And *pirus* means 'pear.'" She paused for a moment as she thought of the huge old pear tree on their farm. She and Katarina would sit in its branches on hot summer days.

"Why are some of the words written in Latin? That's what the priests use."

Mihaela nodded. "Long ago, some priests and monks studied plants. They used Latin for teaching. Now, people use Latin to be accurate about plant names."

"Oak tree is easier."

"I agree!"

"How does Mama know Latin names?"

"She learned from her mother. And Baba learned from a priest."

"Are you going to be a healer, too?"

"I hope so. I'm learning a lot from Mama. And I think I could learn even more if I went to school."

"I don't care if I ever go to school. I can read and write a little. I want to be a farmer when I grow up."

"Then you'll like plants, too."

"But I'll grow crops, not plants."

Mihaela laughed. "Crops are just lots of plants you grow to sell for money. If you're lucky!"

"I want to grow things I can eat." Luka snapped the book shut. "How long until the noon meal?"

"We just finished breakfast!" Mihaela tousled his hair. "You have the biggest appetite of any seven-year-old boy anywhere."

"At least there's enough food for me here. If I eat a lot, someday I'll be big and strong. Like Papa."

"Me, too!" said Blaž.

Mihaela took Blaž's empty bowl to the sink and washed it out. Would Papa stay big and strong if his eyes didn't get better?

The screen door slammed as Mama came in, holding a bunch of small blue-tinged flowers with yellow centers. Fine black dirt clung to their roots.

"Those look like some wildflowers we had in Croatia," Mihaela said. "But the soil on the roots is darker than our dirt back home."

Mama laid the flowers on the table. "You're right, Mihaela. Different minerals and climate could explain the darker soil here." She held the plants up to look more closely. "These are probably native to this area. If they're like the ones back home, the leaves can be made into a poultice to help swelling. But it's late in the season, so there aren't many leaves on the stems. The roots will have to do."

Mihaela studied the flowers carefully. Each plant had many heads and their flowers spread in a ray. She looked in her book to try to find something similar. "Asteraceae?"

Mama looked over her shoulder and nodded. "That's the name of the family for this plant."

Luka laughed. "I didn't know plants had families."

Mama smiled. "Not exactly like our family, but plants can be related. Let's strip the flower heads off. These can also be used as a tonic and tea." She pushed a bunch across the table.

Mihaela picked up a flower stalk and felt little hairs along the stiff stem. She plucked the flower tops and leaves and put them into a bowl Mama had supplied. Luka tried to help, too. The stalks went into a pile.

As she worked, Mihaela couldn't stop thinking about last evening's conversation. Mama had said they would be staying for just a while, but Papa had remained silent. What did that mean?

"Mama, do you remember Valerija?"

"Your friend from the ship? Of course."

"One morning, you had gone up on the deck with the boys and I stayed behind because I was feeling seasick. I heard someone crying, so I went to find out who it was. It was Valerija. She was sad because she missed her home and she hated being on the ship."

"It was difficult for everyone," Mama said.

"She said something else. She told me her mother said people think they'll go to America for a while and then go back to their countries, but no one does." Mihaela hesitated. "That's not true. Is it?"

Mama paused for a long time. "Some people may decide they want to stay, or circumstances make them stay." She reached out to take Mihaela's hand. "I know there are people who have returned. I plan to take you and your brothers and go back to Croatia after Papa's eyes are well. He should return soon, too, because one of his brothers is supposed to take his place."

Mihaela wanted to latch on to every word Mama said, to believe it with all her heart. Mama was always right, she told herself, even as an uneasy feeling remained.

Everything else was changing.

What if this changed, too?

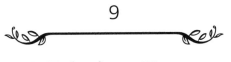

9

A Trip into Town

The sun hadn't risen yet, but Mihaela jumped out of bed at the sound of horse hooves clomping down the road. It had taken Papa two whole days to arrange for borrowing the team from Josip's brother. The poultice they made from the flowers Mama had collected hadn't done much to cure Papa's eyes. Maybe the oil they were going to buy at the store would help. She threw on her clothes and raced out of her room, running hard into Vlado as he was coming down the steps from the boarders' sleeping loft.

"In a pretty big hurry to get somewhere?" he asked.

"Sorry, Vlado. Papa is coming with the horses and wagon."

Vlado's face was blank.

"We're going to the store today."

"Ah, your first trip into town. Calumet is a fine place." He gestured for her to pass in front of him.

Mama was at the boarders' table, pouring coffee.

"Morning, Mama," Mihaela called as she ran out the door. She took a deep breath of the moist dawn air, savoring the scent of pine and damp earth. Papa was approaching with the wagon. Steam rose from the horses' backs as plumes of vapor streamed from their mouths.

"Well, Mihaela, I see you're eager to get going," Papa called out. *"Pauza,"* he ordered the horses, drawing up on their reins.

"Dobro juto, Papa." Mihaela watched the horses bob their

heads as Papa tethered them to a post. She patted one of the horses' flanks. "Horses in Croatia are bigger."

Papa laughed. "There are big horses in America, too. These aren't bred for farm work, like our Percherons at home. They'll do just fine, though." He looked toward the rising sun. "I need to go. The mine foreman doesn't like it if I'm late." His sore eyes almost twinkled. "Now don't spend all our hard-earned money at the store today."

"We won't." Mihaela went back inside.

Mama was stirring a pot at the stove as she turned toward the boys. "Luka, you need to comb your hair." She looked closely at Mihaela's dress. "Is that button about to come loose?"

Mihaela touched one of her dress buttons, and the thread holding it unraveled in her hand. "I can sew it back on."

"We have so much to do today." Mama ladled oatmeal into their bowls. "Eat now, while it's hot. The button can wait until after breakfast."

"Remember the awful porridge on the ship? And the watery pea soup?" Luka added milk and sugar to his bowl, then swallowed a big spoonful. "This oatmeal is so good!"

"Even better than Aunt Ida's porridge back home," Mihaela said.

Mama sat at the table with them and practiced saying the English words on the grocery list that Josip had written for her. "On-yons," she tried.

"On-yons!" the children repeated, laughing.

Mama laughed, too. "You'll learn English faster than I will." She handed Mihaela the list. "Keep practicing. I need to hang the clothes on the line."

"You've already finished the laundry?"

"I knew we'd want an early start." Mama let the screen door slam behind her.

Mihaela swallowed another bite of the oatmeal while she looked at the list. "Ba-con," she tried.

"Ba-con," Luka repeated.

She was glad the English alphabet was almost the same as Croatian. The sounds of some of the letters were different, though.

"Pep-per. Flou-er. O-il. These words feel funny in my mouth." Mihaela giggled.

"On-yons!" Blaž blurted out.

They laughed again.

"Pep-per. The words tangle my tongue," Luka said.

Mama returned. "If you're done enjoying the grocery list, you know what we need to do before we can leave."

The children licked the last traces of oatmeal from their spoons and returned to their chores. When the clock on the mantle chimed ten times, dishes had been washed, beds made, floors swept, and the button sewn.

Mama checked her grocery list and adjusted her shawl. "All right, children. Let's go to town."

Mihaela climbed into the wagon. "Can we check for letters?"

Mama helped Blaž onto the seat beside her. "We'll stop at the post office after the store. I need to mail my letter, too. We could all do with some news from home." She shaded her eyes as she looked up at the sky.

Mihaela saw small, wispy clouds floating against bright blue. "No rain today."

Mama raised an eyebrow. "I hope you're right. I never saw weather change as fast as it does here." She snapped the reins, and the horses began a brisk trot over the rough road.

Distant sounds grew louder as they rounded a bend. Past a grove of trees, the mine entrance came into view. Large carts filled with rocks rolled along tracks that led out of a low building into the shaft of a taller building.

Mihaela could hear loud blasts and the whine of drills coming from inside the mine. She felt their strong vibrations. Last night, she had overheard some of the boarders complaining of sore backs and smashed fingers, and of even more terrible accidents. One man had lost his leg when a drill slipped. Since he was working alone, no one had found him until it was too late. The boarders worried about what would happen to his wife and children. Mihaela shuddered. She wished people didn't have to choose between hunger and danger.

Farther on, they passed a lumberyard. Saws buzzed and the smell of freshly cut wood filled the air. Papa had said there was a lot of building going on to provide miners and their families with housing and other services. The mines were drawing people from all over the world to come work for the good wages being paid. Some miners were even able to save enough money to leave the mines and try less dangerous work. She wondered if that could happen for Papa some day.

Another turn brought them into view of Calumet. It certainly wasn't as big as New York or Chicago, but as they drew closer, Mihaela saw church spires and many other buildings. Some were of red brick, some of wood, and they lined wide streets. Windows with arches reminded her of those she had seen when they had passed through Opatija in Croatia. Many of the buildings had awnings that shielded the windows. They passed livery stables, stores selling furniture, a business with tools and stoves, and several butcher shops. One store had nothing but hats in the window! Mama guided the horses nervously and glanced at a map Papa had drawn for her. "We need to find 213 Fifth Street. Look for a two-story frame building with glass windows on the first floor. That's the business run by P. Ruppe and Son. I hope there's someone there who can understand us."

Mihaela pointed. "I think those are the right numbers." She was glad that numerals here looked the same as in Croatia.

People strolled over fitted planks that ran the length of the street in front of each store. No one needed to get their shoes dirty from horse droppings. Mama pulled the wagon in front of the store and found a post where she could secure the reins.

Mihaela felt nervous but excited. She had never been in a store before. When she opened the door, she heard bells chime. A man in a dark suit with a stiff collared shirt came forward and greeted them. He pointed to his chest. "Joe Alton."

Mama smiled. "Levak." She waved her list.

"Welcome, Mrs. Levak. And children." Then he gestured to the interior of the store.

Mihaela thought his tone was friendly, even if she couldn't understand his words.

Wooden floorboards creaked as they moved to the center of the large space. Lamps gave off a yellow glow of light that made everything in the store easy to see. Her eyes widened and her jaw dropped as she tried to take in the displays of merchandise. Men's and women's clothes were in one part of the store. Hats, caps, and shoes were arranged by different styles and colors. She remembered seeing some well-dressed people at the train depot in New York. There must be some rich people in this town who could also buy such things! Mihaela looked down at her shabby dress and scuffed shoes. She suddenly felt embarrassed.

Mr. Alton led them to a part of the store where the groceries were sold. Rows of cans and jars, barrels and bins with lids, sacks of grain and flour, and bolts of cloth were arranged, stacked, or piled.

Blaž walked with determination toward something on the counter. He pointed to a big jar of peppermint sticks. *"Slatkis!"*

Mr. Alton smiled. "Ah, you've found the candy."

"Can-dee." Blaž was eager to practice more English.

Mr. Alton fished out three candy sticks. He turned for Mama's approval.

She frowned and shook her head. "We can't spend money on such things," she said to Mihaela.

Mr. Alton understood. "My treat." He made a gesture, pointing to himself.

Mihaela tried to interpret for her mother. "I think he said it's free."

"Da?" Mama said. "Thank you," she tried, in thick English.

"You're welcome." Mr. Alton smiled. He handed the first

stick to Blaž. "Can-dy."

"Can-dee!" Blaž repeated. *"Hvala."*

Mr. Alton gave one each to Mihaela and Luka.

"Thank you," they both said, in English.

"You'll be speaking just like the rest of us in no time," Mr. Alton said. "I think we're doing fine here, but maybe I should go and get one of our other employees who speaks your language." He motioned to a sack of grain and patted it with his hand.

Mihaela nudged Blaž as she turned to Luka. "He must want us to sit down there." They took their places on the lumpy sacks and started to lick the candy sticks.

Mr. Alton returned with a young man.

"Dobro juto." He smiled and stuck out his hand. "Franc Dresich."

"Tereza Levak." Mama shook his hand and then handed him her list. The man looked it over, moving among shelves and bins, scooping and wrapping. He chatted with Mama and used a big scale to weigh the flour, potatoes, and other bulky items. Soon the counter was filled, and Mr. Alton started packing things in boxes and sacks.

Mihaela slowly sucked on her candy while she looked around the room. She enjoyed studying everything—bags of grain and cans with colorful labels of pictures and words. As she turned toward her right, something else caught her eye. There, on a shelf across the room, were two beautiful dolls.

Mr. Alton followed Mihaela's gaze. He walked toward the dolls and returned with one of them. He dusted it off with the back of his sleeve and handed it to Mihaela.

Mihaela gasped. She had never seen such a beautiful thing! The doll's head was heavy, made of something like the plates they now used. The hair was painted black and the face had big, blue eyes. Its body, as well as the arms and legs, were soft. Slippers made of black wool covered the feet. The doll's dress was a dense fabric, but not coarse, like Mihaela's. The color was a bright, grass green, with a sheen to it. When she held the doll upright, the dress stood out from the body just enough to show the lacy cuff on the pantaloons below.

Her mother looked over at her and shook her head.

Mihaela knew she mustn't even think about a doll like this. After all, she had Dijana, the doll Papa had carved for her long ago. But how amazing to know that such things could be found right here in this store.

Mr. Alton, Mr. Dresich, and Mama finished their business and began to gather up the provisions. The boys had gone outside, each carrying a small bag.

Mihaela was still looking at the doll when Mama came up to her and took her by the arm. Mihaela handed the doll back to Mr. Alton. *"Doviđenja,"* she said.

"Until next time." He smiled and put the doll back on the shelf, close to the other doll, which was identical but for a blue dress.

Mihaela sighed. She had promised to send Katarina a present, but she knew they'd never be able to afford any of the pretty things she saw here. Then she remembered the most important reason for their trip to the store. "Mama, did we get the oil for Papa's eyes?"

Mama lifted a heavy sack and hesitated, then nodded.

"Is something wrong?" Mihaela asked.

Mama shook her head, but Mihaela noticed her lips were pressed hard into a thin line.

"And what about the mail?"

"The post office is our next stop."

Mihaela picked up the remaining sacks of potatoes and onions.

"See you next time," Mr. Alton said. "Those dolls will be waiting."

Mihaela looked up at the dolls again. She didn't understand everything Mr. Alton had said, but one word stuck in her head. "Dolls," she repeated. That was an easy word to say.

10

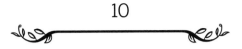

Post Office and Rain

As Mama drove the wagon down another street to the post office, Mihaela looked around her. There were several people walking, but they didn't seem to be in a big hurry like the people in New York. Most of the men wore suits. Some of the women wore long skirts with high-collared ruffled blouses, but there were others who dressed more plainly, like Mama. And everyone was wearing a hat. Mihaela saw her mother reach up and touch her bare head. Would she and Mama be expected to wear such hats, too? They often wore kerchiefs to keep their hair out of the way when doing farm chores, but these were fancy hats with brims and ribbon. She wondered what other customs were different here. And why didn't she see any children her age? There were just a few babies and toddlers with their mothers.

Mama stopped the wagon in front of a small wooden building. "I think this is the post office. Mihaela, can you manage alone in there? I don't want to leave the boys or these groceries." She handed her the letter she had written along with a few US coins.

Mihaela entered the building and tried to remember the writing she had seen at the mail window when they had gone through immigration in New York. She squeezed her eyes shut, picturing the word in her mind. "Let-ter!" she finally said. She showed the man behind the counter the envelope and started speaking rapidly to him in Croatian.

"Letter, I understand." He took the envelope. "Mail this?" He waved it back and forth.

Mihaela nodded.

"All right." He put the letter on a scale. "Postage to Croatia . . . thirteen cents." He held up two hands, squeezed them shut, and then raised three fingers on one hand.

Mihaela handed him all of her coins and he gave her change. She looked at the postman. "Levak?"

He seemed puzzled.

Mihaela pointed to herself and tried to say the new word again. "Let-ter?"

"I get it." He reached into a bin under the counter and took out several letters. "You are a Levak?"

Mihaela nodded.

"Let's see here . . . Banyar, Dresich, Udovic . . ." he read. Looking up, he shook his head. "Sorry. No Levak."

Mihaela's face fell.

The postman shrugged. "Maybe next time."

As she returned to the wagon, Mihaela saw that the blue sky of early morning had changed to a threatening gray. She quickly climbed onto the seat.

"We need to hurry so I can take the wash off the lines before it starts to rain," Mama said. "Hold on tight!"

They were halfway to the cabin when the winds started howling, strange and mournful, through the woods.

Mihaela glanced around uneasily. Mama snapped the reins to make the horses go faster.

A bolt of lightning lit up the sky in front of them, followed by a large roll of thunder.

"Bad noise," Blaž whimpered.

"We can't let these provisions get wet." Mama pulled Blaž close to her side. She flicked the reins again, and the horses started to gallop.

The cabin was in view as rain splashed down in big, fat drops. Mama pulled the wagon to a halt and jumped down to tie the horses. Mihaela and Luka took the biggest sacks and found something small for Blaž. They all raced into the cabin. The rain fell even harder as they returned for another load. Then, leaving the supplies on the kitchen table, they all ran out to the backyard. Thick, wooden clothespins held the heavy mining overalls on the line, but the strong winds had tied the clothes into knots. They struggled to untangle them, then threw the clean clothes into the basket until the skies opened up with a deluge.

"That's enough!" Mama herded everyone into the house.

Mihaela looked through the screen door. "We missed a whole row."

"Those are our clothes." Mama shook her head. "Thank goodness, the miners' things are just a little damp. They won't pay us for wet or dirty overalls. And the flour stayed dry. Now, we need to put everything away."

Mihaela shivered as the wind continued to howl. Unpacking the food reminded her that it was close to noon. By the time they finished, her stomach was rumbling loud enough for everyone to hear. "I need to eat!"

Mama served them reheated beef stew from last night's dinner. She put a loaf of bread on the table, and next to it, a small glass jar filled with a thick, dark-red fruit.

"Mr. Dresich gave us this as a welcome gift. It's a jam made from a local berry that grows in the region."

Mihaela spread some of the jam on the bread. It was both sweet and tart and had lots of little seeds. "Delicious! What's the berry called?"

"I think he called it 'thimbleberry.' He said the fruit is quite small."

"I wonder if it looks like a thimble? Maybe I can look for some around here."

"He said most of the berries are gone by now—either picked by humans or eaten by bears."

"Bears?" Mihaela's eyes widened.

"Bears!" Luka repeated.

"Papa told me there are bears in some of the woods. He said if they ever come near the house, make lots of noise as you run inside."

"I guess I'll be yelling pretty loud!" Luka said.

Mihaela didn't know what to think about bears. "The oil for Papa's eyes," she said between bites. "Is it the right kind?"

Mama hesitated. "It doesn't look as pure as I had hoped. But perhaps it will do."

Mihaela felt her stomach knot up again as she thought about Papa's eyes. She had to find more herbs!

Luka pointed to the window. "Look, the sun's back."

The rain and wind had stopped as suddenly as they had begun.

"Such weather!" Mama frowned.

Luka grabbed Blaž's hand and ran out the door.

The kitchen filled quickly with warm, moist air. Mihaela leaned over to unfasten the buttons on her shoes. Now that they were broken in, she was glad she didn't need to use the buttonhook every time she undid them. She pulled off her shoes and stockings and gratefully wiggled her toes. Barefoot was still better when the days were warm.

Mama started clearing away the dishes. "Mihaela, you'd better go keep an eye on the boys."

As Mihaela stepped out the door, a rag ball hit the side of her head. "Ow!"

"Oops, sorry. I didn't mean for it to hit you." Luka wore his impish grin. "But I guess we're even now for the water you dumped on me."

Blaž wandered toward her. "M'aela hurt?"

"I'm fine." Mihaela rubbed the spot where the ball hit. "I'm supposed to check on you." She threw the ball back.

Luka kicked the ball hard. "I'm big enough to take care of myself."

"Me, too," Blaž said.

Mihaela laughed. "Oh, Blaž, I know *you're* big enough." She made a face at Luka. "Promise to just stay here and not get into trouble? Don't go into the woods."

"Why? Where are you going?" Luka asked.

"For a walk. I won't be gone long." Mihaela went close to the house and called through the screen door. "Mama, the boys are fine and I'll be back soon." Not waiting for her mother's response, she started down the path.

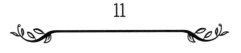

Into the Forest

Mihaela began to skip, then broke into a run. Her bare feet pounded the soggy ground and she pumped her arms hard. She hadn't run since she'd left Croatia. All those days on the ship and then the train. It felt so good to have space and fresh air to move through! At the sound of gulls scolding overhead from nearby Lake Superior, she looked up. All the storm clouds had passed, and the sky was again a deep blue.

The birds' cries were strident and boastful. "What are you bragging about?" she shouted, as they swooped around her. One landed, and Mihaela ran toward it.

Defiantly, it stood its ground and cawed.

"Ha!" she challenged.

The gull flew just a little ahead of her on the road, calling shrilly. Then the bird did it again.

Mihaela ran forward as the gull flew on, while other gulls landed nearby. She wanted to join the game, and she moved farther and farther down the road. Soon, the cabin was a speck in the distance. No other houses were close-by.

Mihaela came to an overgrown wagon track. "Where do you suppose this leads?" she asked her bird friends.

"We know, we know!" they seemed to answer, bobbing their heads as they flew around her.

Mihaela stood still for a moment. She knew she should be getting back to the cabin. But she also wanted to play, even if it was only with birds.

One of the gulls circled closer. "Caw, caw!" It dared her to enter the woods.

Mihaela couldn't resist.

The forest grew densely on both sides of the overgrown path. Birches and evergreens filtered the light into soft beams, and the pine needles made a thick bed beneath the trees.

Mihaela breathed in their fragrant scent. She loved the quiet stillness, broken only by the sounds of her footsteps and the birds in the distance. It reminded her of her secret place in Croatia. As the path twisted and turned, she noticed wildflowers growing in small pockets of sunlight. She stopped to take a closer look. Maybe one of those plants could help Papa.

She bent down and peered at the pools of light. The first revealed mushrooms, but not ones she recognized. She remembered one of her lessons with Mama: *All mushrooms can be eaten, but some only once.* Better not take a chance. Then a small patch of green leaves with long parallel veins caught her eye. It looked like plantain, a plant she knew from Croatia that had many uses. She gently broke off several leaves and put them into her dress pockets. Even though her everyday blue dress had faded to a soft gray, the mended pockets were still sturdy. How she loved having pockets! She could tuck herbs and plants in them, along with any other small treasures she found.

As she turned, she noticed another path beneath the trees that went deeper into the forest. She followed it for a while and came upon a small open meadow. Moths hovered over tall plants with flat white blossoms. She paused to take a closer look. The stalks held tiny flowers in a fuzzy cluster and the green leaves were large and wrinkly. Maybe they would be useful, too. At least the flowers were pretty. She picked several and held them in her hand.

The gulls had stopped calling to her, but now she heard something else. She froze for a minute. Could it be a bear? She was about to cry out when she realized it wasn't an animal noise—it was a people sound. Was there another cabin nearby? Maybe there were children there.

Mihaela quickened her pace. She had to find out.

12

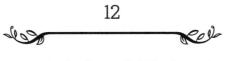

A School Visit

As she edged closer to the sound of voices, she heard a bell ringing. *Clang, clang, clang, clang.* It rang over and over.

She moved toward the direction of the sound. She was at the edge of the forest now and saw a wooden frame building. Mihaela watched from a distance as children swarmed around the door, then scattered. Some were older and some were younger than she was, and a few carried books. A school!

Mihaela waited, watching the children take different routes to go home. She ducked behind a tree as two girls close in age walked past her. Their clothes were different from hers, with more buttons and trim, but they wore their hair in braids, just like she did. What did they learn? Did they get to read a lot? She wondered what it would be like to be with them. Would they be nice and want to be her friends, or would they laugh at her clothes and her lack of English? Her birthday was almost here, and she had no one to tell. Seeing the girls reminded her how much she missed Katarina.

Mihaela lingered. She wanted to peek inside and try to imagine what it would be like to spend her days there. Reading new books and learning the answers to all her questions would be heaven. She found herself taking one small step and then another, inching closer. When she was sure all the children had gone, she tiptoed to a window at the back of the building. Inside, she saw a large room with a wooden floor. Sitting in neat rows were different-sized desks—small ones in the front, larger ones at the back. The desks were made of wood, and a seat was connected to each desk. The larger desks had a bottle of ink sitting on the right side in a little well. Would she ever be able to sit at a desk like that? At the front of the room, a blackboard was covered with white chalk writing, and a red, white, and blue flag hung from a pole in one corner. Shelves holding books lined another wall. All the books were arranged by size and color. She had never seen so many books! What kind of information did they hold? Did students get to read all of them? Her eyes lingered on a large desk that held a pile of papers. When a woman walked into the room, Mihaela froze. She must be the teacher. Could she see her peering through the window?

Mihaela admired the teacher's crisp white blouse and long skirt. Her hair was swept up in a bun and held with pretty combs. As the teacher started to sort the stacked papers, she paused, and then looked toward the window.

Mihaela drew a quick breath.

The teacher hesitated a moment, then smiled and continued sorting papers.

Mihaela exhaled. She struggled to tear herself away. Her family was waiting.

She started back and spotted some wild onions growing near the road. As she tugged on their green stems, the white bulbs came out of the damp ground easily. She grabbed a handful. They were good for remedies and to eat. Mihaela ran home along the path she had followed earlier. She couldn't wait to show her mother the plants she had gathered and tell her about the school. "Mama, look what I found!" she called as she opened the front door of the cabin.

But no one was there.

Bees

Cries rang out from the backyard. Mihaela ran through the cabin and out the kitchen door.

Mama held Blaž on her lap. A wet cloth lay across his forehead while she used a thin piece of bark to scrape welts on his face and neck.

Luka stood nearby, tears streaming down his face. He cradled one swollen and red arm with his other.

"Mama!" Mihaela cried. "What happened?"

"Bees!" Mama started to massage Blaž's chest as he wheezed noisily. "The ball hit a hive. They've both been stung many times. Blaž is having trouble breathing."

Blaž's face was swollen and his lips were tinged with blue.

"Oh, no!" Mihaela looked from one brother to the other.

Luka moaned. "Lots of stings." His right arm was an angry crimson. Mihaela could barely stand to see them. She was supposed to have been looking after her brothers.

"I don't have anything to treat Blaž," Mama said.

The herbs used for bee stings had been lost at the train station. Mihaela dug into her pockets and pulled out everything she had just found in the woods. "I picked some herbs and leaves. Maybe one of these will help." She handed the plants to her mother and looked more closely at Luka. He was covered with fiery welts.

Mama first chose the wild onions. She split the small white

bulbs with her finger, and rubbed them gently over the worst of Blaž's stings. Then she tore up the leaves with the veins—the plantain plant—and gently pushed the pieces inside Blaž's mouth. "Try to chew those, Blaž."

He made a face but did as he was told.

"Mihaela, get me some water."

Mihaela grabbed the bucket and sprinted to the pump. She raced back.

Mama tore up more of the green leaves and chewed them herself, then stuck the pulp on the stings. She chewed more and added water to make a paste, then applied the paste all over the boys' welts. After a few minutes, she put her ear against their chests.

Blaž whimpered, but his breathing had improved a little.

"Here, Luka, you need to chew this, too." Mama helped him with pieces of the plant. "Let's get the boys inside." Mama picked up Blaž while holding Luka by the hand. "They both need to stay quiet. Help me take them to their beds."

Mihaela was eager to do anything she could.

Mama propped up Blaž with pillows behind his back. "Mihaela, sit right by him while I check on Luka's stings. Keep feeding him small amounts of the plant."

Mihaela held one of Blaž's hands in hers while she gave him more of the plant. "Try to chew this, Blaž."

His lower lip trembled. "Hurts."

Mihaela nodded and patted a part of his hand that wasn't swollen. She glanced over at Luka, and saw that his left arm still held many stingers. Mama was trying to remove the stingers by scraping them off with the thin piece of wood. He winced as Mama removed one after another.

Mihaela lifted up Blaž's shirt to check his back. "I think there are a few more stingers left here." She took the piece of wood from Mama and removed them.

"That's good, Mihaela. I'm going to make some more of that poultice. I'll be right back."

Mihaela finished checking Blaž, then walked over to Luka's bed. "I'm sorry you got stung. I should have been there."

Luka shook his head. "The hive was hidden in a tree. The ball hit it and the bees got mad. Bad luck."

"Why did they attack Blaž so much?"

"He was right next to the hive when it fell from the tree. They swarmed him. I ran over to try and make them go away." Luka cringed. "Poor Blaž. He got more stings than I did."

Mihaela looked at all the welts on Blaž. There were several on his neck, some on his ears, and a big red welt just visible under the brown hair on his head.

"Mama got most of the stingers out of him first, because he couldn't breathe."

Mihaela started to cry. "Oh, Luka. I feel awful for both of you!"

Mama returned with more of the poultice and two glasses of water. "Mihaela, why are you crying?"

"I'm sorry about what happened. Maybe if I had watched the boys, they wouldn't have been stung."

"No use talking like that. I am concerned that you went off alone, though, without telling me first. Remember, your father said there could be bears."

Mihaela shuddered.

Mama applied the rest of the poultice to Blaž and Luka, and then gave them each a glass of water. She stayed until both were breathing normally.

"Just lay still now, boys." Mama turned to Mihaela. "Come. We need to talk."

Mihaela followed her mother into the kitchen. The heavy chair made a scraping sound as she pulled it out and sat down. She didn't know what Mama was going to say.

Mama went to one of the kitchen drawers and returned with her pen, the ink bottle, and a piece of paper. She eased onto another chair. "Mihaela, the plants we've been using for Papa aren't working. We need to find something to help his eyes, right away. He told me this morning he can barely see. The oil we got at the store wasn't really what I had hoped it would be."

Mihaela's heart skipped a beat. Mama's face was drawn and taut. Poor Papa!

"The plants you found today are very good, but still not what will cure him. I can't leave the boys now to go search. But you can." She sketched quickly. "Did you see either of these on your walk?" She handed the paper to Mihaela.

Mihaela looked at the drawings. "I'm not sure. Two plants?"

"Yes. Back home, goldenrod grew in open fields." Mama pointed to the first picture. "It has yellow flowers in large clusters on single woody stems. Musk mallow might be along the road, or at the edge of woods."

Mihaela saw that the second plant had five petals in a

funnel-shaped flower. "Is it pink or white?"

"Either color."

Mihaela picked up the paper and put it in her pocket. "Should I go now? Are the boys all right? What about me helping you get dinner ready?"

"I think the boys are recovering. Thank God you found those plants!" She shook her head. "I'll manage with dinner. Take a pot and use a stick to hit it if you hear animal sounds that worry you. Make as much noise as you can to scare things away. Finding these herbs is the only thing that will save Papa's eyes."

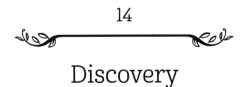

Discovery

Mihaela stepped out the door and ran as she had never run before. Gripping a pot and clutching the paper with the plant drawings, she raced down the road. She kept checking the sketches while her eyes scoured the ground. "Yellow flowers, in the sun," she repeated. "Pink petals, near the woods." She had to find the plants that would cure Papa's eyes.

She paused for a moment while her eyes adjusted from the bright light of the road to the shadows of the forest. She reached down to find a big stick for banging against the pot. Her ears strained to hear anything that might signal a bear as she checked the forest floor. Drooping plants she hadn't noticed before were coaxed up by the slanting rays. Late-afternoon sun filtered through in narrow patches. She moved slowly, careful not to step on anything but pine needles. Earlier, she had noticed wild onions as well as plantain. Now, as she moved from place to place, she saw plants with hairy stems and clumps of fuzzy white flowers. She saw more mushrooms and tightly curled ferns. She saw purple clusters topping thin stems. But not the plants she needed.

As Mihaela moved farther into the woods, she heard her gull friends, high overhead. They were circling about, calling to her. "You're no help!" she shouted at them. "What am I going to do?" She tried another path, then another. The woods were so dense here only small mushrooms poked their spongy heads from the ground. Her breath came in short, quick gasps. These Michigan woods were so unfamiliar!

The gulls had gone and the air was still. She heard twigs snap. An acorn falling, she told herself. Then another snap, louder. Mihaela clutched her pot and stick as her heart skipped a beat. When she heard more crackling snaps, she banged her pot with as much force as she could and moved away from the sounds. She cocked her head once more to listen and saw a flash of black fur moving into the shadows. Her mouth went dry and her heart pounded.

She was scared of bears. She was scared that she wouldn't be able to help Papa. She was scared of this strange new life. Aunt Ida had warned her she would need to be brave to make this trip. But all she could feel inside was a quivering fear.

Scrambling over fallen logs and sharp roots, she turned and twisted until she found a path. Her skin was scratched, and mosquitoes and black flies buzzed around her head.

In the distance, Mihaela heard a whistle. Papa's mine shift was ending and he would be home soon. Her shoulders sagged. What was she going to tell her mother? How could she let everyone down? She retraced her steps as tears burned her eyes.

When she reached the road, she ran again.

Mihaela passed the mine entrance as some of the miners were coming out, and she kept her head down, rushing by them. She never stopped looking for the plants, but her tears made it hard to see.

She slowed when she reached the backyard of the cabin. Walking over to the pump, she splashed cold water on her hot face. Sounds of Mama clanging pans in the kitchen and dinner smells filled the air. The water from the pump cleared her eyes, but her stomach felt like she had swallowed stones. Her chin touched her chest as she gripped tight fists. "I can't give up!" she growled. "I won't!"

When Mihaela raised her head, she noticed a large cylindrical shape lying on the ground at the edge of the yard. It was the beehive that Luka's ball had knocked down. She dropped her pot but held on to her stick and walked toward it cautiously. The hive was cracked open, and something golden was oozing out. She used the stick to check for bees. They had all gone, so she rolled the hive over and found a good way to lift it up. As she crouched to grip the ends, something beneath the hive caught her eye. Mihaela began laughing, crying, and shouting all at the same time. The hive had fallen on a small patch of the yellow flowers she had been looking for. As she looked around, she noticed another cluster growing right at the edge of their yard.

Mihaela's cries brought her mother flying out the door. "Now what's wrong?" Mama called as she ran to her. "What are you doing with that beehive?"

Mihaela scooped up some of the petals next to the hive. "Mama! I ran and ran and couldn't find either of the flowers. Then I saw a bear and I was scared and I came back here so sad because I didn't know what I would tell you. But I saw the hive, and it had honey and the bees were all gone, so I turned it over to pick it up, and look what I discovered!" Mihaela was out of breath. She held out her hand, holding the yellow flowers.

"They're covered with honey. Will that matter? There are more of these right over there, too."

Now Mama was laughing and crying, too. "A bear? Oh, my brave daughter!" She wrapped her arms around Mihaela and hugged her tightly. "And you found the goldenrod right here." Mama shook her head. "I never noticed them beyond that rise. The honey makes it even better. We'll use these flowers and the honey to make a poultice instead of using the oil."

"But I couldn't find the other plant," Mihaela said.

Mama was beaming. "This may be enough. We'll use it on Papa tonight."

Papa walked slowly into the yard. He stumbled over an uneven patch of ground and rubbed his face with the back of his hand.

Mihaela whirled around. "Oh, Papa!" She wiped her eyes quickly before she gave him a kiss on his nose, the only part of him that wasn't covered with dirt. He moved stiffly.

Mama patted Papa on his back and pointed him toward the cabin. "Mihaela found something that we're going to use to treat your eyes tonight."

Mihaela picked up the hive and led her father by the hand.

15

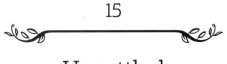

Unsettled

After dinner was over, Mihaela got a bowl and tore the flower petals into small pieces. Mama crushed the honeycomb and strained it through a thin cloth, then added some of the honey and a small amount of hot water to the bowl.

Papa settled into his usual chair in the kitchen. He winced as he tilted his head back. "Is this really for my eyes, or do I get to eat it?" He tried to smile.

"It's for your eyes first." Mihaela soaked a strip of cloth in the mixture.

"Smells nice." Papa sighed as Mihaela applied the strips.

Luka stood nearby, watching. He edged toward the bowl and stuck his hand in it. "Mmm," he said, licking his fingers.

Mama moved him away gently. "This is for Papa's eyes."

Luka scowled. "Can't I have some? If I hadn't hit the nest with my ball, you wouldn't have any honey."

"You're right. And you suffered for it, too."

Luka flinched as he looked at his bee stings.

Mama cut small slices of bread and spread a little honey on them, handing one each to Luka, Blaž, and Mihaela. "We just can't eat all the honey before we see if it will help Papa's eyes."

Blaž pushed his bread away. "Don't want honey. Bad bees." His welts were still red and swollen.

Mihaela put her arm around her little brother. "Poor baby."

Blaž stuck out his lower lip. "Not baby. Big!" Then he

burst into tears.

Mama picked him up. "Oh, Blaž. Your stings must hurt a lot." Finding another bowl, she mixed the leaves Mihaela had found earlier with water and applied fresh paste to Blaž's welts. "Better?"

Blaž's lip was still sticking out, but he nodded.

Mihaela lifted the first cloth strip from Papa's eyes and applied a freshly soaked one. She repeated this until all of the solution was gone. "Should we make more?"

Mama moved toward Papa, looking closely at his eyes. "No. I think that's enough for tonight. Take a strip and rinse it with hot water. Then gently wipe Papa's eyes one more time."

Please let this help Papa, Mihaela prayed.

"Blaž, I think you'll feel a lot finer after a good night's sleep. You too, Luka." Neither boy protested as Mama led them to bed.

Papa turned to Mihaela. "I've been thinking of how you used to read to me back home in Croatia. Did you bring the Bible?"

Mihaela nodded.

"Would you read to me tonight? I've missed that."

"Of course, Papa." She remembered explaining to Katarina that reading to Papa was one of the things she could do for him. She went to retrieve the Bible.

When Mihaela came back, Papa and Mama were doing the dishes together.

"What would you like to start with?" Mihaela asked.

Papa put down a pot he was drying. "The Psalms, I think. Psalm 40."

Mihaela found the page and began to read in a low voice.

When she finished, Papa bowed his head and was quiet for a moment. "Now you pick something."

Mihaela was preoccupied. She couldn't settle on any passage, and her eyebrows knit together in a frown. "Hmm . . ."

"What is it?" Papa asked.

Mihaela looked up. "I like the Bible, but I wish we had a book about the sun, too."

"What do you mean?" Mama asked.

Mihaela rubbed her forehead. "Remember the night we got here? How we noticed that the sun set later here than in Croatia?" Mihaela pressed. "How does the sun work? How does it rise and set every day?"

Papa shook his head.

Mihaela drew a deep breath. "I saw a school today. Maybe I could learn those things if I went to school."

There was a long silence.

Papa looked first at Mama, then at Mihaela. "Your mother's been a fine teacher for you, and she needs you to help her with all the chores . . ."

Mama interrupted. "And once Papa's eyes are better, we'll all be going back to Croatia."

Papa shifted his weight from one foot to the other but said nothing.

Mihaela saw that her parents looked as confused as she felt. Why couldn't there be clear answers to things! She set the Bible on the table, ran into her room, and flung herself down on the bed. She feared what Valerija had told her on the ship was true—they were going to stay. What would that be like, spending her life in Michigan? Would she ever be able to go to school or have friends? Would she have to do chores for the boarders until it was time for her to get married? Since Katarina was a little older, she had warned her that things might change for her when she turned twelve. She would know soon enough. Tomorrow was her birthday. She could never have imagined the changes were going to be like this.

16

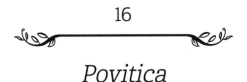

Povitica

Rain beat a steady rhythm on the roof all night. Mihaela tossed and turned. She slept fitfully until the clock chimes from the next room woke her. A new day—her birthday. It felt like big changes were coming. She just wasn't sure what they would be. "Maybe some things will be better, Dijana." She arranged her doll against the pillow. "I want to hope."

Papa was standing at the stove when Mihaela walked into the kitchen for breakfast. As he turned around, she gasped. The swelling on his eyes had subsided by half. "Oh, Papa!" She threw her arms around his neck.

Papa patted her on the back. "I'm keeping my fingers crossed, but it's been a long time since my eyes have been this good." The mine whistle blew, and he gave Mihaela a kiss. "We'll have much to celebrate tonight. Happy birthday, daughter!" He waved as he stepped out the door.

Mama had a huge smile on her face. "Happy birthday, Mihaela."

Mihaela's head was spinning.

"The plant combined with the honey made all the difference," Mama said. "You have learned well. You see with your eyes and your heart as well as your brain."

Mihaela was overjoyed. Ever since she had lost the basket of herbs at the train station, she was afraid it would be her fault if Papa's eyes didn't get better. "I'm so happy I found a plant that's helping Papa!"

"You are becoming a gifted healer, Mihaela." Mama beamed.

Mihaela felt relieved. Relieved and proud.

Luka and Blaž stumbled into the kitchen, rubbing sleep from their eyes.

"Papa's eyes are getting better," Mama said. "Mihaela found a plant that's working. And today is her twelfth birthday."

"Hooray!" Luka cheered. "Hooray for Papa, and hooray for Mihaela." Then he shook his head. "But I'm still only seven."

Mihaela laughed and gave him a hug. "Don't worry, you won't be seven forever. You're growing fast."

Mama filled their breakfast plates with bacon and pancakes. She gave the pitcher with maple syrup to Mihaela first.

Mihaela poured the thick amber liquid from the pitcher and watched the stream glisten as it dribbled down the stack of pancakes. A good birthday breakfast.

Luka covered his pancakes with syrup, too. "Will we have a party?"

Mama started getting out bowls and the big sack of flour. "Tonight. But first, we are going to make something special. I can't make it a surprise since I need everyone's help. *Povitica*."

Mihaela remembered the last time they had eaten the special bread—their picnic by the side of the road as they traveled to the ship. "But it's so hard to make. I thought you had to have a lot of people."

Mama looked at the children. "Your aunts and I probably teased a little about how hard it is." She smiled. "We are four strong people. After everything else we've been through, making *povitica* should be easy. We'll make extra dough, so there will be enough for us and the boarders."

They began as soon as the breakfast dishes were done.

Mama put yeast into a small bowl and added warm water. Mihaela broke open fat walnuts, cracking their shells with a heavy frying pan. She separated the nutmeats and put them into a metal grinder with a handle. As she turned the handle, the sharp blades ground the nuts fine and the bits fell into a glass jar attached beneath the grinder. So many walnuts to grind!

Mama measured out cups of flour into a big bowl and added eggs, sugar, and a few other ingredients. The boys broke up sticks of cinnamon. They took turns using a club-shaped wooden tool to crush the spice in a small bowl.

"Smells good," Blaž said.

"Mihaela, do you remember what else goes into the filling?" Mama asked.

"Yes! Sugar, eggs, and a little milk." Mihaela found the other ingredients and mixed them with the cinnamon in a separate bowl.

Mama stirred the foamy yeast mixture into the flour. She mixed it and then moved the dough to the table. She sprinkled a little flour and started to push the dough with the heel of her hands, out and back. As she flipped it over on itself and started the motion again, she turned to Mihaela. "Would you like to try?"

Only the adult women in the *domaćinstvo* were allowed to knead this dough.

"Yes!" Mihaela dusted her hands with flour and sank them into the warm dough, grasping it firmly. The springy feel was a new sensation, and she pushed it the way she had seen Mama doing it. Out, back, flip. Soon, she had a steady rhythm. After a while, the dough became more elastic.

"Just right." Mama placed a damp cloth over the top of the bowl. "Now the dough has to rest for a while. But we can't." The daily chores were still waiting. They cleaned lamps, swept the floor, and hung laundry while the bread dough rose.

Mihaela worked all morning. As she passed through the kitchen, she saw the cloth on the bowl had risen, and she lifted it to peek at the spongy dough beneath. The yeasty smell took her back again to the *domaćinstvo*. She wondered what Katarina was doing right now, and thought about her aunts and uncles. She sighed as she lowered the towel. She wished that she could celebrate her birthday with them, too.

Mama stopped to check the rising dough. She pressed the dough down just as the clock struck twelve. Time for lunch. By the time they finished their meal, the cloth over the bowl had risen above the rim.

"Time to knead again?" Mihaela asked.

Mama nodded. She punched the dough down in the bowl, kneaded it a little more, and spread a large cloth over the table. Then she divided the dough into three balls. She sprinkled a little flour on the cloth and placed the balls on top of the cloth. "The cloth will help us turn the dough," she said, as Mihaela retrieved a heavy wooden rolling pin.

Mama rolled the dough out, and Mihaela brushed it with melted butter. Then she added the filling mixture. The children turned the cloth and helped Mama roll the dough into oblongs.

They trimmed the *povitica* to fit into greased loaf pans to rise one more time.

Mihaela had watched with Katarina the last time the aunts made the pastry. Memories overwhelmed her. She missed her cousin, her family, and her home more than anything in the world. She tried not to cry, but couldn't help it. "Sorry, Mama . . . my birthday . . . making *povitica*. I miss everyone so much! I'm glad Papa's eyes are getting better. But if I can't be back home, then I want to learn things. Except you don't have time to teach us here, and Papa says I can't go to school because there's too much work . . ." She felt like a well had opened in her heart. More tears fell even as she tried to stop them.

Luka hung his head. "I miss home, too."

Mama wrapped a floury arm around Mihaela. "Remember how often we were hungry in Croatia? We have enough to eat now. Your father and I had a long talk last night, after you children were in bed. He thinks we may have a chance for a better life here. You know that the farm is no longer able to feed everyone . . ."

"You mean we're never going back?" Mihaela cried.

Mama hesitated. "I don't know. Papa thinks we should stay for a while. I miss home, too. This is not the life I expected." She gave a heavy sigh.

"What's going to happen to everyone?" Mihaela began. Her heart was breaking.

Mama turned back to face Mihaela. "We'll talk with Papa about everything tonight."

17

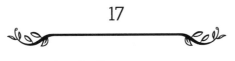

Birthday News

Mihaela trudged to her room and reached for her book of herbs. She drew a picture of the plant she had found that helped Papa's eyes and made a note: *Mix goldenrod petals with honey and use as a poultice.* Then she picked up her doll. "Well, Dijana, I guess Valerija was right. We are not going back to Croatia anytime soon." She was glad to have a doll, even if she was twelve now. Who else did she have to play with or talk to? No friends, no cousins . . . she lay back on her pillow. She was exhausted from crying and thinking about all the changes in her life. She dozed off for a while until a sweet odor roused her. The *povitica* was done.

"Are you feeling better now?" Mama asked.

Mihaela shook her head as she walked into the kitchen.

"Would you like to go find more herbs? Would a walk make you feel better?"

"Right now?"

"Yes. Enjoy yourself, but stay out of the woods and don't be too long."

Mihaela found her shawl and a basket. Some fresh air might help. She took a pot, then added a wooden spoon, too. That could make more noise than a stick.

She followed the path near the road and noticed leaves were already turning to gold and crimson. It was early September, but she didn't remember seeing this much autumn color around her birthday in Croatia. A brisk wind blew at her back, and she pulled her shawl a little tighter. Wild carrots with the purple floret in the center of the lacy flowers were good to eat, so she yanked some out of the loamy soil and put them into her basket. Her feet crunched on acorns as startled squirrels jumped out of her way. "Plenty of food for all of us here," she said to them. She wished that were true at home for her hungry cousins. When she heard the mine whistle blow, she turned back.

Mama was working at the stove. "Did you find lots of good things?"

Mihaela put her pot and basket down. "Mostly wild carrots."

"We'll use them in tomorrow's soup. Can you go get the boys? Papa and the other men will be here soon."

Mihaela found her brothers sitting on their beds. Luka hid something behind his back.

"What have you got there?" Mihaela asked.

"Nothing."

Blaž giggled. "A secret."

Mihaela tried to smile. "It's almost time for dinner." She held out her hand to Blaž.

"A secret!" Blaž said in a loud whisper.

Mihaela helped Mama with the final preparations for dinner. She put bread and slices of *povitica* into baskets and then set the tables. Luka came to the kitchen hiding something under his shirt.

The men started to arrive, and Mihaela looked for Papa. His familiar laugh rang out as he walked down the road and entered the house with some of the boarders.

"There's the birthday girl," Papa boomed. He gave Mihaela a kiss, and then a bigger one for Mama.

Mihaela looked at his eyes. "Papa! Your eyes are even better!"

"Daughter, I believe you have found my cure."

Mihaela's heart swelled with pride. So much depended on Papa getting better.

Papa bowed his head as he took his place at the table. He was silent a long time before he finally said the blessing, then added, "Lord, we thank you for our health."

"Amen." Mihaela kept her eyes closed while she offered thanks for Papa's improving condition. She could finally put the lost herbs behind her. When she looked up, she saw a steaming platter in front of her. "*Sarma!* We haven't had this since Croatia." She grinned when she realized Mama had sent her out looking for herbs so that she could surprise her with her favorite dish: sour cabbage leaves filled with ground beef, bacon, rice, and onions.

Mama smiled as she served. "For your birthday, Mihaela."

"We have something for you, too." Luka pulled out a folded sheet of paper. "Blaž and I made this for you."

She took the paper from Luka and saw a circle with two eyes and a smile, and two long lines for legs. She looked at Blaž. "Did you draw this for me?"

Blaž nodded. "Myself!"

Mihaela opened the card. In large letters were the words *Sretan Rođendan*. She looked at Luka. "Good writing! *Hvala*."

Luka had signed his name and Blaž had made a squiggle.

Papa pulled an envelope from his shirt pocket. "I have

something, too. But your mother needs to read it first. Vlado went to the post office today." He handed the letter to Mama.

"At last!" Mihaela cried. "Is there something for me from Katarina?"

Mama held the envelope to her chest for a moment, then opened it with shaking hands. She scanned the pages quickly, and a smile softened her face. She handed Mihaela a sheet of paper.

Mihaela drew a deep breath. She had waited a long time for some word from her cousin.

Dear Mihaela,

I miss you so much. I'm better at milking than before, but it's not as much fun without you. I haven't been practicing my writing. Can you tell?

And I still don't like to read as much as you! How is Michigan? I hope your birthday is a happy one.

Your loving cousin,

Katarina

Mihaela felt a stab in her heart when she saw the drawing of two girls sitting in a pear tree included in the letter.

Mama was quiet as she read the letter from Aunt Ida.

Papa raised his eyebrows. "What's the news?"

Mama shook her head slightly, and her smile faded.

Papa paused for moment, then looked at Mihaela. "I'll have Mama read the letter to me later. It's your birthday, Mihaela, and my eyes are getting better thanks to the plants you found. So we need to celebrate. How about some music?"

Mihaela nodded but she still felt a little sad. "Of course, Papa."

"Luka, tell Josip to get his fiddle," Papa said. "We'll join everyone after we're done."

They finished the last bites of *sarma* and *povitica*, cleared the dishes, and washed the pots and pans.

Then Mihaela stepped out into the main room.

All the boarders were assembled, and Josip held a box tied with a big, red ribbon. He presented it to Mihaela. "From all of us boarders."

Mihaela took the box and sat down on one of the log chairs. She untied the ribbon and lifted the lid. There inside was the beautiful doll with the green dress from the store.

"*Sretan Rodjendan!*" the boarders cheered.

"Oh!" Mihaela couldn't find the words for more. To think she would own such a beautiful thing! She loved Dijana and wouldn't abandon her. But this was the finest doll she had ever seen. The boarders were almost as nice as her uncles.

Josip smiled. "We all chipped in a little."

Mihaela lifted the doll out of the box. "Thank you! Thank you!" she said. In English.

Everyone laughed. Papa stepped forward, holding his *tamburica*. "*Sarma* from your mother. A special card from your brothers. And a wonderful gift from the boarders. Now it's my turn. Actually, from both your mother and me."

Mihaela held her breath. So many things had changed. What was next?

"You like to learn," Papa began. "You know a lot about plants.

And you want to know about everything else. What I'm trying to say is, you've convinced us that you should go to school."

Mihaela's breath caught again. "Oh, Papa! Mama!"

Mama beamed.

Papa continued. "You have to speak more English before you can start school, so it may take a while. Josip said he would teach you. Until then, you'll still have to help Mama. Some of your aunts and uncles and cousins will be able to join us soon, and then we can share the work here in Michigan like we did in the *domaćinstvo*."

"So Katarina will come?"

Mama nodded.

"And I get to go to school?" Mihaela could barely take in everything she was hearing.

"Yes, eventually," Papa said.

Mihaela swallowed hard. She already knew this new life wasn't easy. But if they weren't returning to Croatia, having Katarina and the others come here was the next best thing. And a chance to go to school! She stood up a little straighter.

She had survived so much already. She had always hoped her life could get better. Now she knew it would.

"*Hvala!* I mean . . . thank you!" As she whistled the tune Papa was playing, she grabbed her two brothers by the hands. "Now we have reasons to dance again."

The structure over a mine shaft, a shaft-rockhouse (possibly the south range) with flowers in the foreground.

Five men working near a rock pile, shaft-rockhouse in background.

Copper miners with their lunch buckets. Some are boys.

A car full of miners prepares to descend.

Miners at work. Calumet and Hecla underground—
Osceola Amygdaloid.

The Ingersoll Drill advertisement in *The Portage Lake Mining Gazette*, 1883. An artistic rendering of a one-man drill operation.

Underground scene of miners preparing to drill in the Osceola Mine.

Postcard with artistic rendering of a woman readying dinner
(peeling vegetables) on the back porch in Calumet, MI.

A group of people on the corner in Calumet with storefronts
visible in background.

P. RUPPE
& SON,

General Merchandise

213-217 Fifth St., Calumet, Mich.

Established 1869.

Dry Goods, Clothing, Furniture, Hats and Caps,
Shoes, Gents' Furnishings.

We Handle the Best Groceries

That Money Can Buy.

A Full Line of the Celebrated F. Mayer Shoes
for Children.

Sole Agents for "Queen Quality" Ladies
Footwear.

Advertisement for a general store on Fifth Street in Calumet, MI,
listing some of the merchandise sold and its date
of establishment (1869).

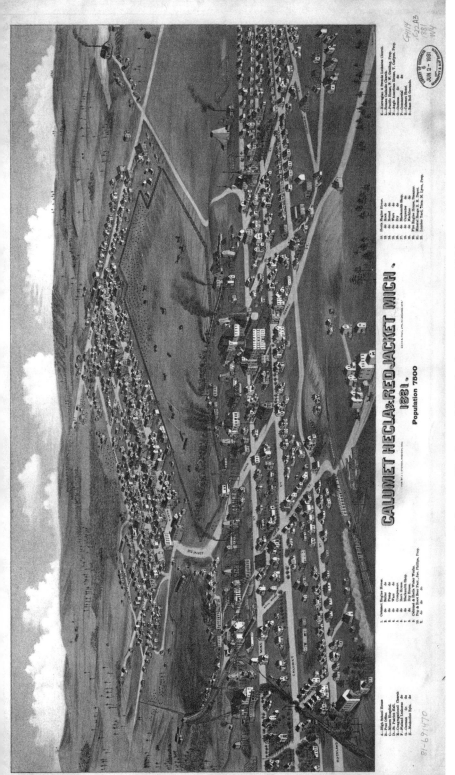

Calumet, Hecla, and Red Jacket, Michigan, 1881.

My Family's Recipe for *Pasties*

(Four generous servings; recipe can be doubled)

Pie Crust:
2 C. flour
2/3 C. + 2 T. vegetable shortening
4–5 T. cold water
1 t. salt

Measure flour, salt, and shortening into a bowl. Blend with a pastry blender until solid. Add water and mix until flour is moistened and dough begins to gather together. Scrape bowl and divide dough into two balls. Flatten the balls into rounded discs. With a floured rolling pin, roll dough out until each disc measures approximately 10" in diameter. Cut each disc in half so you have four portions of pastry crust. (Save a little dough before you roll it out if you want to try to make the braided edge, as mentioned in the story.)

Pasty Filling:
Pasty filling can be a subject of discussion in the Upper Peninsula. Some argue it has to have one ingredient but not another. In my family, it had to be diced sirloin, not ground beef, and never any carrots, but always rutabaga. What goes into a pasty has become a tradition unique to each family.

1 pound raw sirloin steak, cut into small dice
1 small peeled rutabaga, diced
1 medium peeled potato, diced
1 small onion, diced

Mix together and season well with salt and pepper.

Divide meat mixture into four portions. Place meat filling in each of the four pasty discs, leaving apprx. 1/4" margin from edge, and fold crust over. Crimp edges with your fingers or a fork, or add the braided dough rope and press to attach.

You can pierce the top of the crust with a fork to let out steam. (In the late 1800s in Michigan, the baker would mark the initials of the miner to identify his pasty.)

Place pasties on a cookie sheet and bake in a preheated oven at 425° oven for 15 minutes, then lower heat to 350° and bake an additional 25 minutes. Let pasties sit for five minutes before serving.

My Family's Recipe for *Povitica*

(Approximately 10 or more servings)

For the dough:
1 1/2 C. warm milk
1/2 C. sugar
1 t. salt
2 large eggs, at room temperature
1/4 C. softened butter or margarine
2 packages dry yeast
1/2 C. warm water
7 C. all-purpose flour

In a small bowl, dissolve yeast in warm water and let sit until foamy, apprx. 10–15 minutes.

In a separate large bowl, combine the warm milk, sugar, salt, eggs, and butter.

After yeast has foamed, add to the larger bowl and mix all together.

Add half of the flour and mix until smooth. Add more flour until the dough becomes easier to handle. Knead dough on a lightly floured surface until smooth. Put dough in a greased bowl, cover with a damp cloth, and leave in a warm place until doubled in size, about one hour.

Once the dough has doubled, punch down and then let double again. Divide the dough into three parts. Roll out each part into thin rectangles.

For the filling:
2 C. finely ground walnuts
1 C. sugar
1 t. cinnamon
1/2 C. softened butter or margarine

Mix the walnuts, sugar, and cinnamon together. Brush the butter on the rolled-out dough. Sprinkle the mixture over the surface of the dough. Roll each rectangle into a tight log, and trim to fit either a greased loaf pan or a greased cake pan, using three pans total. (For cake pans, arrange the dough in a circle.) Cover, and let rise again. Then bake at 350° for 30–45 minutes, depending on pan size, until a toothpick inserted comes out clean.

My Family's Recipe for **Sarma**
(Serves 6)

Ingredients:
1 large head green soured cabbage*
1 pound browned ground beef (drained of grease)
1 pound ground cooked ham
6 slices cooked bacon, crumbled
1 C. partially cooked rice
1 medium onion, diced
2 T. olive oil
1/2 t. garlic powder or 2 cloves diced fine
1 egg, lightly beaten
1 t. salt
1 t. pepper
2 quarts sauerkraut
1 C. tomato sauce or 1 can tomato soup

Preparation:
Rinse the sauerkraut, if very salty, with water and layer approximately one-third of it on the bottom of a large roasting pan or casserole. Set aside. Cook the onion in the olive oil until lightly browned. Add onion to a mixture of the ground beef, ham, crumbled bacon, rice, and egg. Stir to combine and season with salt, pepper, and garlic.

Take a small amount of the meat mixture and place it in the middle of each cabbage leaf. Roll the leaf lengthwise and tuck ends in so that the mixture is secure. Place the rolled *sarmas*, seam side down, in the casserole on top of the sauerkraut. Alternate *sarmas* and additional sauerkraut, ending with sauerkraut. Pour tomato sauce or soup on top and cover. Bake at 350° for 1 1/2–2 hours.

*There are different ways to "sour" cabbage. You can core a fresh head, place it in a large pot of water, add 1–2 T vinegar, and boil for 10-15 minutes, or until cabbage leaves are soft. Another way to sour or ferment the cabbage is with salt, but that can take 4–6 weeks. Whole sour cabbage leaves are also available for purchase through the Internet.

Recommended Books for Young Readers

Bierman, Carol. *Journey to Ellis Island*. New York: Hyperion-Madison Press, 2005.

Bunting, Eve. *Dreaming of America*. New York: Troll/Bridgewater Books, 2000.

Burr, Dan, and Ruth Hailstone. *The White Ox*. Honesdale, PA: Calkins Creek-Boyds Mill Press, 2009.

Castaldo, Nancy. *The Story of Seeds: From Mendel's Garden to Your Plate and How There's More of Less to Eat Around the World*. New York: Houghton Mifflin Harcourt, 2016.

Curtis, Rebecca S. *Charlotte Avery on Isle Royal*. Mount Horeb, WI: Midwest Traditions, Inc., 1995.

Elster, Jean Alicia. *The Colored Car*. Detroit: Wayne State University Press, 2013.

Cushman, Karen. *The Midwife's Apprentice*. New York: Sandpiper, 2012.

———. *Rodzina*. New York: Yearling, 2005.

Giff, Patricia Reilly. *Lilly's Crossing*. New York: Yearling, 1997.

———. *Maggie's Door*. New York: Yearling, 2003.

———. *Nory Ryan's Song*. New York: Delacorte, 2002.

———. *Water Street*. New York: Wendy Lamb Books, 2006.

Harlow, Joan Hiatt. *Star in the Storm*. New York: Aladdin Paperbacks, 2000.

Hart, Allison. *Anna's Blizzard*. Atlanta: Peachtree Publishers, 2005.

Kadohata, Cynthia. *Kira-Kira*. New York: Atheneum Books for Young Readers, 2005.

Karr, Kathleen. *Man of the Family*. New York: Farrar, Straus and Giroux, 1999.

Lasky, Kathryn. *An American Spring: Sofia's Immigrant Diary*. New York: Scholastic, 2004.

Levine, Ellen. *If Your Name Was Changed at Ellis Island*. New York: Scholastic, 1993.

McMullan, Kate. *For This Land: Meg's Prairie Diary*. New York: Scholastic, 2003.

Mobley, Jeannie. *Katerina's Wish*. New York: Simon and Schuster, 2012.

Paterson, Katherine. *Day of the Pelican*. New York: Clarion/HMH Books for Young Readers, 2009.

Peterson, Cris. *Birchbark Brigade: A Fur Trade History*. Honesdale, PA: Calkins Creek-Boyds Mill Press, 2009.

Reeder, Carolyn. *Captain Kate*. Bethesda, MD: Children's Literature, 2006.

Royston, Angela. *Life Cycle of a Mushroom*. Chicago: Heinemann Library, 2009.

Schröder, Monika. *The Dog in the Wood*. Honesdale, PA: Front Street-Boyds Mill Press, 2009.

Swain, Gwenyth. *Hope and Tears: Ellis Island Voices*. Honesdale, PA. Calkins Creek-Boyds Mill Press, 2012.

Taylor, Sydney. *All of a Kind Family*. New York: Bantam Doubleday Dell Books for Young Readers, 1989.

Thompson, Gare. *We Came Through Ellis Island*. Washington, DC: National Geographic Society, 2003.

Vanderpool, Clare. *Moon Over Manifest*. New York: Random House, 2011.

Wearing, Judy. *Fungi*. New York: Crabtree Publishing, 2010.

Wilder, Laura Ingalls. The *Little House* books. New York: HarperCollins, 2004.

Annotated Bibliography

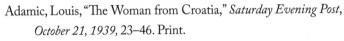

Articles/Magazines

Adamic, Louis, "The Woman from Croatia," *Saturday Evening Post, October 21, 1939,* 23–46. Print.

This article was written about my great-grandmother and her family and their experiences leaving their Croatian village and settling in Michigan. The author had interviewed her and other members of that generation in the 1930s. I found only two errors in Mr. Adamic's research, having to do with the actual arrival date of the ship and the age of my grandfather, who made the trip with his mother and an older brother. (The author may have done this intentionally, honoring their privacy request.) His location information, however, was so accurate I was able to find the unmapped ancestral village based solely on his writing.

Whittier, Frank C., ed., *Portage Lake Mining Gazette,* March 4–September 9, 1886. Microfilm.

General information regarding daily life through the lens of a weekly newspaper "issued in the interest of mining, blast furnaces, manufacturing and the general welfare of the whole Lake Superior region." Railway timetables, weather reports, advertisements, local news, etc.

Books

Anderson, George E., and Richard E. Taylor. *Images of Rail: Copper Country Rail.* Charleston, SC: Arcadia, 2008.

Catton, Bruce. *Michigan: A History.* New York: W. W. Norton and Company, 1984.

Catton, Bruce. *Waiting for the Morning Train: An American Boyhood.* Detroit: Wayne State University Press, 1987.

Memories of the author's childhood in Northern Michigan.

Chermayeff, Ivan, Mary J. Shapiro, and Fred Wasserman. *Ellis Island: An*

Illustrated History of the Immigrant Experience. New York: Macmillan, 1991.

Cleland, Charles E. *Rites of Conquest.* Ann Arbor: The University of Michigan Press, 1992.

Daniels, Roger. *Coming to America: A History of Immigration and Ethnicity in American Life.* 2nd ed. New York: Harper Perennial, 2002.

Desnick, Harvey. *Blooming Seasons.* Calumet, MI: Cordifolia Publishing, 2009.
Color photos taken by the author along with notes of Keweenaw Peninsula wildflowers and herbs blooming from spring-fall, used for identification and accurate descriptions.

Dunbar, Willis F. *All Aboard!: A History of Railroads in Michigan.* Grand Rapids, MI: W. B. Eerdmans, 1971.
Chapter 7, "The Northlands and Its Railroads."

Dunbar, Willis F., and George S. May. *Michigan: A History of the Wolverine State,* 3rd rev. edition. Grand Rapids, MI: W. B. Eerdmans, 1995.
Chapter 18, "The Mining Boom," details the importance of copper to the Upper Peninsula.

Harrison, Lorraine. *Latin for Gardeners.* Chicago: University of Chicago Press, 2012.
Reference source for plants with correct Latin and common names.

Henderson, Troy. *Lake Superior Country: 19th Century Travel and Tourism.* Chicago: Arcadia, 2002.
Good photos with captions showing period dress, railroads, and nature.

Hubbard, Bela. *Memorials of a Half-Century in Michigan and the Lake Region.* New York and London: G. P. Putnam's Sons, 1887.
Collection of essays describing Michigan's geography, geology, and local history that mentions the UP's long daylight in summer.

Johnson, Rebecca L., et al. *National Geographic Guide to Medicinal Herbs.* Washington, DC: National Geographic Society, 2014.

Lankton, Larry. *Cradle to Grave: Life, Work and Death at the Lake Superior Copper Mines.* New York: Oxford University Press, 1991.

——. *Hollowed Ground: Copper Mining and Community Building on Lake Superior, 1840s–1990s*. Detroit: Wayne State University Press, 2010. Details and insights about communities of mine workers and their families.

March, Richard. *The Tamburitza Tradition: From the Balkans to the American Midwest*. Madison: University of Wisconsin Press, 2013. History of the tamburitza, based on a dissertation at the Folklore Department of Indiana University.

Taylor, Richard E. *Houghton County 1870–1920*. Charleston, SC: Arcadia, 2006. Images of people, buildings, mines, and transportation.

Tekiela, Stan. *Wildflowers of Michigan Field Guide*. Cambridge, MN: Adventure Publications, Inc., 2000.

Thurner, Arthur W. *Calumet Copper and People: The History of a Michigan Mining Community from 1864 to 1970*. Hancock, MI: Book Concern Printers, 2002.

——. *Strangers and Sojourners: A History of Michigan's Keweenaw Peninsula*. Detroit: Wayne State University Press, 1994. Background information about various ethnic groups that lived in the Copper Country.

Correspondence/Scrapbooks

Houghton-Portage Township Schools, Houghton, MI. Notes to the author, April 2004. Correspondence about educational history and building information from the nineteenth century. Timelines, photographs, and an unattributed report (n.d.) titled, "History of Houghton-Portage Township School District." Also included was a photocopy of "History of the Schools of Portage Township in the Copper Country" from *Michigan History Magazine*, 1917–1918.

Lucas, Anthony. Scrapbooks, circa 1906–1960. Private collection of letters, newspaper clippings, and photographs compiled by my grandfather (originally Anton Lesac/Lesic), born January 2, 1880, in Smisliak, Croatia, chronicling his life as an immigrant, Michigan state legislator, prosecuting attorney, and judge.

Lucas, Robert. A. Letter to the author, October 28, 1993.

Correspondence with Robert A. Lucas, second cousin, who shared recollections and copies of family photos, including one of the ancestral home in Croatia.

Maps

Gale, M. P. *Geological Survey of the Upper Peninsula of Michigan 1869–1873*. New York: Julius Bien, 1873. Print. Ann Arbor: Bentley Historical Museum.

Historic reference document, showing information relating to the mines of the area.

Haefer, F. C. Bird's-eye view map of Houghton, MI. 1881. Postcard reproduction. Ann Arbor: Bentley Historical Museum.

Official Records

National Archives and Records Administration (NARA), Washington, DC. *New York Passenger Lists, 1820–1957*. Provo, UT: Ancestry.com via stevemorse.org. Web archive.

I located the manifest with my great-grandmother and my grandfather's names listed that documents the ship they boarded. This information helped me research what the ship looked like, their departure port, and what foods they served on board.

National Archives and Records Administration (NARA), Washington, DC. United States Selective Service. Draft card of my grandfather, Anthony Lucas, verifying his birthdate. Microfilm.

Web

Bradley, Sherri. *The US GenWeb Project*. http://www.usgenweb.org/research/immigration.shtml.

Genealogy research portal with helpful recommendations about finding immigration and passenger arrival records.

Center for Upper Peninsula Studies. "U. P. History." Northern Michigan University, Marquette, MI. http://www.nmu.edu/upperpeninsulastudies/node/16.

Portal for many aspects of Michigan's Upper Peninsula, including history, folklore, mining history, political history and geography.

Central Pacific Railroad Photographic History Museum. "Locomotives and More." Web archive. http://cprr.org/Museum/Locomotives/index.html

Resource for descriptions and details of railroad engines and cars used in the United States during the mid-late nineteenth century.

Cook, William. *Michigan Forests Forever: Teacher's Guide*. Michigan State University Extension; Forest Biomass Innovation Center, Escanaba, MI. http://mff.dsisd.net/Default.htm.

Tree basics, including identification, forest ecology, and environmental concerns.

———. *Upper Peninsula Tree Identification Key*. Michigan State University Extension; Forest Biomass Innovation Center, Escanaba, MI. http://uptreeid.com.

This site is a child-friendly reference for both trees and plant identification and shows particular counties in the Upper Peninsula where species grow.

Copper Country Historical Collections. *An Interior Ellis Island: Ethnic Diversity and the Peopling of Michigan's Copper Country*. "Keweenaw Ethnic Groups: The Croatians." Michigan Technological University Archives. J. Robert Van Pelt Library, Houghton, MI. ethnicity.lib.mtu.edu

Information about the various Keweenaw ethnic groups, including Croatians.

"Destination America." http://www.pbs.org/destinationamerica/usim_wn_noflash_4.html.

Accompanying website for a PBS-produced television series about immigration.

Houghton County Historical Society. http://www.houghtonhistory.org/exhibits.html.

Keweenaw County Historical Society. http://www.keweenawhistory.org/sites/sitemap.html.

Johnson, Dan, et al. "Bringing the Past to the Present." *The Keweenaw Ingot.* Summer 2005. National Park Service, US Department of the Interior. https://www.nps.gov/kewe/learn/news/upload/2005KeweenawIngotfor-web.pdf.

Juch, Juden, and Roy. "My Zeisler Family." http://www.juch.net/zeisler.htm. Information about immigrant ships leaving from the port of Bremen/Bremerhaven, Germany, in the late 1800s, which is the port from which my ancestors departed. Descriptions of life onboard and a few photos.

Keweenaw National Historical Park. "Keweenaw's Copper Story." US National Park Service. http://www.nps.gov/kewe/index.htm. The role of copper in the lives of the people who have lived in the Upper Peninsula, from ancient native peoples to the many immigrants who came to work during the boom years. History, photos and multimedia.

Keweenaw Time Traveler. Regional historical maps and other historical resources for the Copper Country. http://www.keweenawhistory.com.

Magnaghi, Russell M. *Portals to the Past: A Bibliographical and Resource Guide to Michigan's Upper Peninsula.* http://www.nmu.edu/sites/DrupalUpperPeninsulaStudies/files/UserFiles/Files/Pre-Drupal/SiteSections/UPHistory/Upper_Peninsula_Bibliography.pdf.

Michigan's Copper Country in Photographs. Keweenaw Digital Archives. J. Robert Van Pelt and Opie Library, Michigan Technological University. http://digarch.lib.mtu.edu. Original photographs of the Calumet-Houghton region from the late 19th century, accessible online.

Michigan History Center. http://www.michigan.gov/mhc/0,4726,7-282-61080---,00.html.

Michigan's Internet Railroad History Museum http://www.michigan-railroads.com/RRHX/Timeline/1880s/TimeLine1880sBackUp.htm.

Norway-Heritage Hands Across the Sea. http://www.norwayheritage.com. Information about passenger ships from a variety of ports in Europe in the late nineteenth century, including photographs and other historical data. (This site allowed me to find a picture of the ship that brought my ancestors to the United States, the Lake Simcoe of the Beaver Line, formerly registered as the EMS from the North German Lloyd shipping line.)

"The Peopling of America." The Statue of Liberty-Ellis Island Foundation, Inc. http://www.libertyellisfoundation.org/peopling-of-america-center. A timeline showing forces behind immigration and their impact on the immigrant experience.

Powell, Kimberly. *Castle Garden–America's First Immigration Center.* http://genealogy.about.com/od/ports/p/castle_garden.htm. Portal to database, history, immigrants, passenger lists.

Tamburitza Association of America. "Overview of Tambura Instrumentation." http://www.tamburitza.org/TAA/articles/instruments.html. Illustrations and definitions of the various acoustic stringed instruments in the tambura family.

US National Park Service. *Castle Clinton.* www.nps.gov/cacl/index.htm. Site features information and photos of the immigrant entrance point used prior to Ellis Island, where my family was processed before entering the United States.

Image Credits

p. vi Mihaela's Journey. Map by Coni Porter.

p. 101 MS 042-045-U-194, J.T. Reeder, photographer; Reeder Photographic Collection, Michigan Technological University Archives and Copper Country Historical Collections, Houghton, Michigan.

p. 102 MS 042-039-T-071, J. Harry Reeder, donor; Reeder Photographic Collection, Michigan Technological University Archives and Copper Country Historical Collections, Houghton, Michigan.

p. 102 MTU Neg 00558, Roy Drier Photographic Collection, Michigan Technological University Archives and Copper Country Historical Collections, Houghton, Michigan.

p. 103 ACC 239-5-6-1985-02-124, Frederick Fraley Sharpless, photographer, Eric Sharpless, donor; Frederick Fraley Sharpless Photographic Collection, Michigan Technological University Archives and Copper Country Historical Collections, Houghton, Michigan.

p. 103 MS003-011-GN101.1, Universal Oil Products, donor; Calumet and Hecla Photograph Collection, Michigan Technological University Archives and Copper Country Historical Collections, Houghton, Michigan.

p. 104 LD3328H3-18-1, Raymond Smith, donor; Centennial Collection, Michigan Technological University Archives and Copper Country Historical Collections, Houghton, Michigan.

p. 104 ACC 239-5-6-1985-02-127, Eric Sharpless, donor; Frederick Fraley Sharpless Photograph Collection, Michigan Technological University Archives and Copper Country Historical Collections, Houghton, Michigan.

p. 105 No neg 2010-11-01-13, "L. D. H," artist. Postcard c/o Greenlee Printing Co, Calumet, MI. Postcard Collection, Michigan Technological University Archives and Copper Country Historical Collections, Houghton, Michigan.

p. 106 Nara 42-139, J. W. Nara, photographer, William Nara, donor, Nara Photographic Collection, Michigan Technological University Archives and Copper Country Historical Collections, Houghton, Michigan.

p. 106 Book E726-M6-08-01, Archives Book Collection, Michigan Technological University Archives and Copper Country Historical Collections, Houghton, Michigan.

p. 107 Henry Wellge, Beck and Pauli, J. J. Stoner. Library of Congress, Geography and Map Division. J. J. Stoner. Madison, WI: J. J. Stoner 1881. http://hdl.loc.gov/loc.gmd/g4114c.pm003401.

Acknowledgments

I would like to thank the following people for their assistance in making this book a reality:

My husband, Bill, and children Elizabeth and Nicholas, for their extraordinary patience and participation during research trips and the entire writing and revising process; my Treetops writing group—Amy Appleton, Monica Baker, Peter Fakoury, Peter Fendrick, Traci Grigg, and Jane Udovic, for years of encouragement and help; Mary Quattlebaum, for her friendship as a teacher, mentor, and early believer; Carolyn Coman, for her workshop magic as well as extra support; Lindsay Hiltunen and Georgeann Larsen of Michigan Technological University Archives and Copper Country Historical Collections for their help obtaining photos and permissions and for cheerfully answering questions; Thomas Truscott, member of the Michigan Historical Commission and former history teacher, for his encouragement and early enthusiasm; Silvija Belajec and Zana Pedic, advisors to the executive director of EDS19, World Bank Group, Washington, DC, for Croatian translation and expertise with pronunciation and spelling; John Backman of Dollar Bay, Michigan, for sharing photographs, resources, and local knowledge; Jennifer Strand, Osceola Township School/Public Library, for sharing "A History of Osceola Township"; Jeremiah Mason, archivist at the Lake Superior Collection Management Center, Keweenaw National Historic Park, for his suggestions and in-depth knowledge of the Copper Country; Ellen Braaf, regional advisor for SCBWI, who has helped me and so many others in our mid-Atlantic chapter; and the children's librarians at the Georgetown and Palisades branches of DCPL.

Special thanks to Kathryn Wildfong for editorial support, guidance, and kindness, and her terrific team at WSU Press—Carrie Teefey, Emily Nowak, Rachel Ross, Kristina Stonehill, Jamie Jones, and copyeditor Lindsey Alexander.